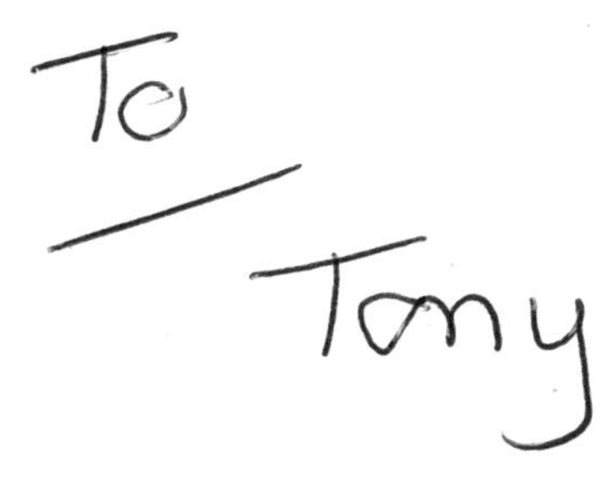

Fallen Angel

By

George Hauton

Sincere best wishes from George
Haworth, December 15th
2013

ISBN: 978-0-9570205-0-4

Printed in England by:

Bakes & Lord, 529 Beacon Road, Bradford

Published by George Newell Hauton, 1 Woodfarm Cottage, Sykes Lane, Saxilby, Lincoln LN1 2PB

For Susan

Chapter One

Because of me, and indeed the authority of my work, do folks from all over the globe congregate in my little village high up on the Yorkshire Pennines in the false hope of seeing me go about my heavenly business. Sadly for them I do not, and cannot, offer such a reward for their endeavours. Some would admit, perhaps, they have espied one or more of my famous family and indeed even spoken with the same; but I fear it is all nonsense, and such folk of indeterminate sanity should be avoided or, at best, smilingly excused for their eccentricity. A few others, more serious-natured folk, with the gift of thought-transportation - to you, the Reader of this tale, they are known as 'psychics' - tend to keep their gift to themselves and only impart their thoughts to those whom they can share a trust in. In all respects, none so far have crossed the barrier of life and death to detain me in conversation, as such, though they may claim vociferously to have done so. So I must strongly impart on you, the dear Reader of this tale, that I walk unseen amongst the hordes of excited but misinformed people who rush to Haworth to lay claim to having spoken to a Brontë. None of their claims hold any foundation, no matter how earnestly they desire it. So, with that in mind, please now accompany me as we take a journey around my village. I shall begin our adventure at one of the best times of the year in Haworth: the colourful season of Christmastime. It is perhaps the coldest time also, but I do not feel the vagaries of the weather anymore, my spirit form offering me protection from even the vilest of the Pennine weather that lesser mortals in real life must suffer and endure.

It is barely nine in the morning as I rise up from my slumbers; outside the lattice the weather is drear and misty, the dark graveyard looking sinister in the early light of December. It may surprise the Reader of this story to know that I do not reside in my 'official' resting place beneath the cold flagstones of St. Michael's church, nor indeed, the vault I was placed in with the rest of my family, save for dearest Anne who was interred at Scarborough her beloved town by the ocean. Folk, it would seem, imagine I am down there slumbering and indeed many flowers are placed over the tomb to indicate such sentiments; but my soul, like my sister Emily's and brother Branwell's, is up and about and away from the confines of the vault, and only our pitiful bones remain imprisoned there until the end of time. I cannot vouch for the whereabouts of my dear sister Anne as she is not with us, and never has been, since the Angel of Death took her, but I suspect she is, even now, happy and joyful at being able to walk along the beach at Scarborough. Branwell, of course, is placed discreetly where he was always to be found: in the Black Bull public house! The times my poor father went in search of the rascal only for the latter to escape through a rear window and repair back to the Parsonage with all haste! There were always keen eyes ready to warn my wayward brother of Papa's approach, indeed, the regulars delighted in the game of hide and seek and found great amusement in the angry redness of their parson's face when he realised he had been duped yet again! By the by, back to my own story now.

I pass through what is now commonly known as 'Charlotte's Room', and descend the stone staircase just as the keeper of the shop takes a tray containing hot drinks and biscuits to the staff working in the library. I decide to follow her through and listen in to the conversation. The smaller of the two ladies manning the library, is giving a colourful account of something she has read in the newspaper about a local man apprehended by the Constable for being in possession of drugs. I tut-tut to myself and agree entirely with the sentiments of the other portly librarian about the state the village is sinking into. Nevertheless, if it wasn't drugs in my day it was alcohol abuse and fornication with willing members of the opposite sex, which was the cause of many of my Papa's angry outbursts. Where he was trying to bring goodness and the love of God into the lives of his flock, it seemed that most – if not all – turned their backs to his ministry, instead revelling in the sins of the flesh, debauchery and drink. I think that is the sole reason why Papa strictly forbade us to go out into the village and gain friends. Even our school days were never conducted here, as you, the Reader, will well know. Haworth village in the mid-1800s was a terribly vile place to live, most especially for its sanitary defects, but more of that later. I return now to the library situation to size up the newest staff member, a young lady carrying the drinks tray, who has come to work at the Parsonage gift shop. This is her third week and the poor creature professes how much she loves her new employment to the two librarians. I do not believe she would enjoy such rapturous thoughts if she had to live here in my day, with no modern machines, or running hot water, or amazing electricity. There was nothing more hateful than rising from a snug bed on a freezing winter morn and having to boil water to bathe in, the only reasonably warm room being the kitchen. One did not loiter in these toiletries in such harsh weather conditions!

I leave them to their idle chatter and walk through to the silent gift shop. As yet, not all of the staff have arrived, most of whom work flexible hours of a temporary nature. The shop itself does not open until after ten in the morning and besides, Haworth is a ghost town at this early hour.

Unlike the streets outside, and in the village centre, the Brontë Parsonage Gift shop is not blessed with colourful Christmas decorations, save for the odd bit of tinsel in the display window. I do not know whether this is attributed to frugality on the part of the present owners of the museum, or whether it is deemed inappropriate for such extravagance in these prudent times! By the by, I would find it most pleasing if the whole effect was made more inviting to the unwary customer about to extinguish part of their hard earned income on 'Brontë souvenirs' or books attributing to the same at an extortionate cost! In that respect, it would be deemed money well spent at this time of year.

I briefly look in at the silent office, the hub of the museum, where most decisions – good or bad – are made. I do not wish to apply either praise or condemnation on the present officers of the Brontë Society, but I would end this topic with a warning to those who run my former home: the eyes of the literary world are upon them!

Outside, in the early morning bleakness of a foggy December, I trace my steps past the high wall of the Parsonage garden, with the Sunday school opposite, and enter St. Michael's church. I leave the latch untouched as I glide in, regardless of newly erected doors or walls, my long Victorian dress and petticoats sweeping the stone flags. I am surprised to find I am not alone at this hour: a young woman, heavily cloaked against our winter weather, is writing something on a little scrap of paper. I watch her intently as she tearfully straightens up, turns, and places the precious slip of paper onto a branch of the 'prayer tree' next to her. It is a modern creation whereby mourners, and others with sentimental interests, can leave heartfelt notes about their loved ones and let the Sunday service congregation pray for them and their heirs at an appropriate time. When I and my family passed from this life, there were no such offices to offer prayers for us. I found the experience with the sorrowful young woman very touching. Perhaps her Christmas will now be much happier for relieving her thoughts and sadness into the arms of others, who knows? In any respect, I quietly leave the lady's side, she totally oblivious of my presence. I fear that had she become aware of me, she would be rendered unconscious on the stone floor, struck by convulsions of the heart. I would have dearly loved to have been given the opportunity to embrace that sad lady and to tell her she was not alone altogether in the world, but it is beyond my power to intervene. So I quietly excuse myself from the church and walk down the narrow lane by its darkened sides, and come to the flight of steps by the Black Bull public house. I pause and look around me. No other living creature, save for a black and white cat sat by the entrance to the nearby White Lion Inn and engrossed in grooming itself, disturbs the barren scene, and yet within the next half hour the street will be transformed into a busy thoroughfare by the day's tourists.

Quietly I descend the steps, daintily lifting the long hem of my dress. I laugh to myself in carrying out this most mundane of exercises and wonder why I bother doing it: my spectral clothes can no longer be soiled by the filthy streets that once were old Haworth. Indeed, Main Street is scrupulously clean, apart from the occasional bit of litter that some unfeeling individual cannot be bothered to place in a bin. I decide to wander over to the Tourist Information Centre, once the home of the Yorkshire Penny Bank, and, above that, the first Brontë Museum. Inside, a vivacious, smartly dressed young lady is going along tidying the racks of books, humming a well known Christmas carol to herself, no doubt content in her employment. I note her beautiful figure but the skirt she is wearing is far too short for modesty's sake! I do declare selfish and crude men may willingly find her attractive and burden her with lewd and suggestive comments. I believe the young lady knows she is beautiful, and will not give in to my urges to make herself 'more respectable'. Pah! the folly of youth.

I hold her under careful observation a little longer before I venture back onto Main Street, my intention to seek out other prey for my sarcasm. I do not have long to wait: up the steep hill come a laughing couple, both in their early-to-mid fifties I should imagine. One of them, the lady, has a distinctive American accent, while her escort speaks uncommon English. These two could be very interesting, me thinks! I allow them passage, deliberately following them at a discreet distance. Suddenly, the woman stops and turns around,

"Hell, I reckon someone is following us!" she cries out in alarm, but her male companion tells her not to be so silly. I stiffen and come to a halt: perhaps this woman is a psychic and I have become unmasked! My heart begins to race as the American lady looks keenly in my direction, but I need not have feared, the moment passes and they resume their taxing walk up the steepness of Main Street. I continue after them, intrigued by this odd couple. I wonder if they are married, or merely good friends. The holding of hands might indicate the former, but seconds later, a chill runs through me when the lady says she fears that her husband is sending someone over from the States to check up on her. Aha! An illicit union I declare: now I really must follow and report my findings back to my sister Emily! I very soon have my chance as the couple settle on the Villette Coffee Shop cafe, and he orders refreshments whilst the lady sits at a table by the window. I quickly join her and sit directly opposite. In time the man returns with drinks and food, and placing a tray on the table he sits opposite his lover, their hands reaching out over the table and entwining.

"Sex was great last night," he beams.

She tells him to keep his voice down even though no one else, apart from the serving girl, is present. I feel myself colouring as the man unfolds more lurid details of their previous night of mischief! I am shocked rigid; this couple are so open about their relationship, surely someone must overhear their claims and take note? But no-one seems to care in your modern world anymore, and morality died out long ago. If it had happened in my day, the couple would have become outcasts, and shunned by everyone they met. I do affirm unlawful liaisons did occur amongst the population, but it was done in utter secrecy, I may add! This present couple had no scruples. I became very embarrassed when they began to discuss in much greater detail, acts of physical love, that, strange to lesser mortals, "turned them on," as they smilingly reassured each other. To add insult to their unsuspecting marital partners, they were wondering what to buy them from Haworth as a gift for Christmas!

I do declare I was livid with this couple and rose to leave, determined I would not tolerate this situation a moment longer, and vowed never to see them again. Unfortunately, they were to cross my path again in the not too distant future!

Chapter Two

Still smarting from my involvement with the lawless pair, I made my way down the steep hill known as Butt Lane, which eventually leads down to Haworth railway station. Halfway down, I decided to turn right and go sit in the splendid arboretum park; even in the coldness of winter, it offered seclusion and shelter from the elements. Though still a foggy day, the short grass of the immaculate lawns still held their lush bright green vegetation, posing a stark contrast to the misty and dismal weather. Lower Haworth was hidden in the fog, and behind me I could only just make out the dark buildings of Main Street. My dear sister Emily loved this prospect, the drear weather and the coldness; nothing seemed to satisfy her more than walking out into the fog and losing herself on the wild expanse of the heath about our village. She claimed the moors were at their best in adverse weather, hiding the lost souls of thousands of Haworthians who had lived and died before us. Emily probably saw her Heathcliff and Cathy dancing through the foggy uplands, but for myself it used to send shudders through me even just venturing out on a foggy night to our privy in the back yard; one imagined all sorts of demons out there watching one's every movement! Matters were made even worse by the close proximity of the nearby churchyard with its 40,000 inmates thus interred. If one wishes to be frightened out of their wits, then a walk through a pitch black cemetery at dead of night is thoroughly recommended! Even when I were alive, I detested being out alone in the darkness of the graveyard, like on the many occasions Papa sent me on errands to the Black Bull to retrieve Branwell from the clutches of drink!

This morning though, in the park – which was never here in my day – I sat down on a metal bench and contemplated the strange couple I had just had the misfortune to meet. From what I could gather their love affair, be what it may, was conducted in a stranger fashion than even the participants! Both claimed it was a good thing they had met, through being members of the Brontë society, but bemoaned the fact that they could meet up only twice a year to carry on their relationship. I find it extremely difficult to imagine how a love affair could survive such a long period of absence, both interested parties being on the opposite sides of the Atlantic

Ocean! I must admit, I admired their staying power, but at the same time condemned their actions of betrayal to their relevant spouses. Even if both their marriages were without love or warmth, they were doing wrong in the eyes of God. I just hoped they would not see fit to enter church for the morrow's Christingle service, and thus insult our Lord still further!

They disturbed me much, this couple, but I was powerless to intervene and I suspect I would receive severe admonishment if I did! The lady caused me some great anxiety though, feeling she suspected a spirit form of some description was hounding her like a ravenous wolf hot on the trail of its prey. I must be careful, maybe I will walk in front of them if I again suffer the misfortune and indignity of crossing their paths. Haworth is but a small community compared to Keighley, so I felt it very likely I had not seen the last of the irksome pair.

I rose from my seat and decided to walk downhill and stand on the platform of Haworth railway station. I loved the sight and sound of the steam trains, although quite a rarity in my day, as the railway had not long been in evidence in our part of the world after I passed on; indeed, it did not reach Haworth or Oxenhope until long after I had departed your world. Now, at this time of morning, the station was deserted of folk save for a gentleman behind the pay kiosk, engaged in conversation with a man I took to be an engine driver - judging by his sooty and oily clothes and black cap proclaiming he was a member of the Keighley and Worth Valley railway. I edged closer to get a drift of their conversation.

"Bit dead at t' moment, innit son?"

"Aye. It's still early yet though Sam, I expect things will pick up shortly," replied the man sat behind the kiosk window. The grubby engine person – for I know not what rank of service he held – sniffed and popped himself against the counter.

"My lass Peggy and her cousin Laura are showin' their Aunt Polly around t' Parsonage tomorrow, afore goin' t' kids Christingle service int' church. They're mad ont' Brontë's."

"And you're not, I take it?"

" You're dead right I'm not... It's all got out of hand just int' last few years; strangers from all over coming and drinking our beer and eatin' our grub. Why, half on 'em never buy nowt, just come to see if they can spot t'Brontë lasses."

"At least it's keeping us in a job, eh Sam?"

"Aye, that's as maybe, but I still think t'Brontës ought to have stayed in Thornton... Haworth is busier than Keighley... we can't do with all these off-cummed-un's cluttering our streets up."

"We got taught Brontë's at school 'til it were coming out of our ears Sam," complained the man behind the glass.

His unkempt companion agreed, and suggested my family were nothing but trouble-makers! I was furious and wished in that moment I could have flayed the pair of them with a horse whip: how dare they talk about us in such a callous way!

I decided I had heard enough of the despicable pair and went at once out of the building and back over the old wooden footbridge. I made haste up the steepness of Butt Lane, its severe incline bothering me not as my spirit form sped with ease over the stones. It had lately begun to snow and now the flakes were coming down heavy and thick. A long cold winter loomed for Haworth and its inhabitants, but in that moment as the snow whirled in a white fog around me, all I could think of were the way our once-proud family were looked upon by the working class folk of Haworth. If it were not for us, those two individuals back there at the station would be seeking employment frantically; and if it were not for my family, Haworth would be a desolate, silent, inhospitable and bleak community. I hoped those two men would suddenly realise just how fortunate they were to have the likes of us place bread in their mouths and that of their families, and last but not least, help place brass in their pockets. Yorkshire folk are renowned for being gruff and careful with their money, but to bite the hand that feeds you leaves me in a confused state. It is best I depart and find someone who is genuinely concerned about the welfare of my village, and of course, who really loves our family.

By now, the hour was past eleven, and already yonder Main Street was filling up with the day's visitors, all eager to enjoy the spirit of Christmas in a village made famous by us. As I glided onto Main Street I noted several young ladies attired in bonnet and Victorian costume, all of whom looked very becoming. I could tell at a glance they were not of my world, just three Misses dressed up to lend an air of nostalgia to the streets of Haworth. Several folk, including a young Japanese girl of about twenty years of age, had stopped the young ladies and were taking photographs of them. I drew beside the unsuspecting Oriental girl, and listened intently to her conversation.

"Please... you are the three sisters, no?" she asked, having taken her precious pictures and studying her subjects most keenly.

"Nay, love," replied one young lady, her voice broad Yorkshire. "We're part of t' celebrations for Christmas... we're t' do with t' tradesman's guild. We're paid to dress up like this."

"Oh," smiled the Japanese lady, curtly inclining her head. "It is good you make effort to please tourists," she beamed, "I am from Nagato, in Southern Japan... I travel many air miles, but it worth every yen to be here."

"You're a big fan of the Brontë's, then?"

"Very much so; I wish I could see the ghosts of the famous sisters, I have been told that honourable Parsonage is haunted... see, I have given coloured photograph by stranger to prove this thing."

The three young ladies eagerly crowded round the diminutive Japanese lady, all excited to hold the picture. I too, slipped between them and was most taken aback with what I saw thereon. The front door of the Parsonage was shown, and there, in the light from behind, stood a female figure dressed all in black. Although the figure was blurred, it was quite obviously a woman with a billowing dress. I recognised her immediately!

"Upon my soul, it is Tabby Ackroyd, our former cook and housekeeper!" I cried.

Of course, the four ladies were unaware of my voice and presence amongst them, and went on to speculate whom it may or may not have been. Finally, the leader of the three British ladies, a very tall girl in her twenties, dismissed the photograph as a fake, and proclaimed loudly that there were no such things as ghosts. The silly young hussy! How keenly she would have retracted her statement, had I the audacity to suddenly find form and reveal myself before her and her laughing companions! The Japanese lady looked quite sad about it all, and slowly walked off after thanking them for their time. I caught up with her and accompanied her up the street.

"Fear not," I soothed, placing my spiritual arm around her thin shoulders, "there is life after death, you must ignore all claims to the contrary, my dear." Of course, my pleas fell on deaf ears and I withdrew from her a little as we slowly made our way forward amongst crowds of people. That is the strange thing about Haworth: the place rises as a ghost town and yet within the space of two hours one is obstructed at every step of the way by strangers who seemingly have elicited themselves from thin air!

Suddenly, I notice another young lady - this time an English Miss – lift up her right arm and shout across my little Japanese friend in greeting, from the midst of a crowd.

"Makinoto! Over here! Thank God I've found you, where did you wander off to?" she said, breathless, as she hurried over and linked arms with her special friend.

"I walk to bottom of street... take pictures of three girls dressed in fine costume, they very nice but did not believe in my ghost picture."

"Never mind, love. I expect most folk you speak to won't believe either."

"And you also, Andrea?"

"Me? Oh. I tend to keep an open mind," laughed her friend.

"Wise child," I nodded approvingly.

The two of them wandered off into the crowds of folk; I chose not to follow on this occasion. Instead I purposefully walked into the Black Bull to look once again at the old rocking chair said to have been used many times by my brother Branwell. I was quite annoyed every time I espied it, for the true chair was at this moment languishing inside the Parsonage – where it had for many a year – the one at the Inn was a mere replica. It may fool the inhabitants of the Inn, but I think it is rather sad for those wishing to view real Brontë relics. Still, I can do nothing about the situation and the noise emitting from the lounge is too much for my poor ears, so I repair forthwith to the questionable quietness of Main Street once more. I note that it has stopped snowing, but the setts on the street are very treacherous to the unwary, and I fear for the elderly visitors, especially the ladies. I'm afraid Haworth will not escape the white tumult this year. In previous seasons only hard frost has graced the roads and rooftops, and some Decembers have been uncommonly mild with heavy rain rather than snow. We shall see.

I decided to free myself of Haworth and go for a short sojourn to the nearby moors, using West Lane as my route. Vehicles of all shapes and sizes go by, throwing up great quantities of brown looking slush. I would have been most annoyed if I had yet been alive and been the unwilling recipient of this highway filth. Once clear of the last building in Haworth I steer myself towards the rocky summit of Penistone Hill, via Dimples Lane. In my day, this snow-covered hillside was swarming with workers trying to earn a meagre living for their families. A great quantity of yellow-black grit-stone was mined from here, most of it used in the building of hundreds of dwellings in Haworth and its immediate locality. Now the workings lay silent under a blanket of snow, the men, machines and buildings all long gone. The valley floor has been levelled flat, and it is hard for me to recall how it used to look. I briefly turn my attention to the spinning wind turbine on the eastern hillside above Haworth, and the one remaining stone quarry still in existence. I find it most displeasing that such a monstrosity can be erected here, but the situation is not as bad as in Oxenhope, where a whole battalion of those weird contraptions stand sentinel, like soldiers. Had it not been for the splendid efforts of the Brontë Society and other interested parties, the whole of the Worth Valley would have been infested by windmills! I salute the brave efforts of the folk who were willing to stand up for the rich heritage my family have brought to our rude hills and valleys of the Western Pennines. My dear sister Emily was appalled when she espied the very first contraption being built on Oxenhope Ridge, although it has to be said that initially she was quite interested thinking it was to be a modern landmark for her fellow moors lovers, like Stoodley Pike, that overlooks the distant Hebden Valley. However, her mood quickly changed when she saw the first sail being lifted into place. Those poor men who were employed on the project must have had melted ears from the things my volatile and fiery sister was calling them – in epithets too crude to tell you the Reader! But now the irksome machines are here, and I daresay they will remain for a number of years.

I pass through the swing gate of Haworth New Cemetery, just below Penistone Hill, my task to visit the grave of a lady aeronaut by the name of Miss Lily Cove. The unfortunate Miss met her death over Stanbury Moor, when she leapt from a hot air balloon and her parachute failed to open in time. Now she lies buried, almost forgotten, under the soggy peat and mud of Haworth soil. I have seen Lily on numerous occasions, but she never ventures far from her grave. She is always to be seen weeping and holding her head in her hands, the trauma and stress of what happened to her on the fateful Gala day never leaving her. Her superior, a Captain Bidmead, who was also from London, quickly forgot about Lily and soon found another female willing to take her place. I believe the lure of money far outweighed his sentiments for poor Lily! Should one wish to visit Lily's last resting place, they can hardly miss it: the headstone is of a drab blue colour and portrays a balloon on its face. The grave is directly in front of one as they proceed up the cemetery road from the swing gate. There are a few other old graves but mostly the resting inhabitants of this silent field passed away long after I did, and a lot of the headstones are of your generation.

There are no human footprints in evidence as I walk over the snow, indeed, neither are mine! The only sign of life are various bird tracks and the paw prints of a solitary fox. Again, the snow begins to fall as I leave the cemetery and make my way daintily back down the hill to Haworth. The sky is now ink-black, and the light is already fading, even though the afternoon hour is barely past one. Darkness comes early to this hill country and only the brave or the foolhardy remain in its barren wastes at their own peril.

I receive a shock as I walk across the car park to my old home: the loving pair I have so deftly tried to avoid were even now entering by way of my garden gate! What sacrilege! I fumed inwardly as I caught them up, giving anything to be able to close the front door in their faces. But then cold reason threw something in mine! Was it not I who was desperately in love with my married Belgian schoolmaster, M'suir Constantin Heger? Were it not I who had besieged him with many passionate love letters once I had returned to England from my years of frustrating work with him, first as pupil, then as teacher? Only he did not reciprocate my love. My letters were torn to shreds. His dutiful wife secretly retrieved them from a waste bin and meticulously sewed them all back together again for future historians to browse and conjecture over. Mine was a one-sided love affair, doomed to failure; Constantin thought more of his family's affections than mine, and I was cast out into the darkness like a leper, without hope or mercy. So what right had I to condemn this couple? I believe I was jealous of them!

I followed the couple at some considerable distance, should the lady of the party detect my presence and whirl round like on the last occasion.

This time though, all was well, and she seemed to have eyes only for her lover. I tried to imagine I had taken her place and it was M'sieur with me as I guided him around my former home. What would Papa have made of it all, had it really happened?!

Eventually, I tired of this cat and mouse game and left them to it, making my way slowly down the stairs to the gift shop. I paused to look out of the landing window over the billowy whiteness of the deep snow outside; already the sky was turning darker towards evening, the short winter's day nearing its conclusion.

Soon it would be Christmas time with all its attending bouts of joy, bickering and overeating. Our family were no different to our modern day counterparts in that we had many family conflicts over the festive period, no doubt mainly brought on by Papa's refusal to let us do anything constructive. Even outdoor play was refused on Christmas Day when we were children. Church was deemed more important, both in the morning and evening. Thus passed one of the most important dates on the calendar; we were expected to sit and play quietly with our new toys or other Christmas gifts. Boxing Day was more relaxed and we were allowed to go out with the servants for a long walk on the moors, weather permitting. I note in your day, children are rarely seen walking or doing any sort of physical exercise to strengthen their young limbs, preferring to stay indoors to work their electrical gadgets. Our only source of indoor enlightenment was to stand and sing around our old piano. I have seen and heard your modern television or music centres and I do not like either, my poor head would become deafened with the noise of such eccentricities. On one occasion whilst I was stood unnoticed on the pavement of West Lane, a young man drove slowly by in his car, from within came the loudest boom-booming of a drum I have ever heard... and all one continuous tune! Gracious me, the fellow must be tone deaf!

Back to reality, I make my way through the snow to Main Street once more, and it is there that I make a startling discovery. Outside the door of the Black Bull, a young man is engaged in a fierce quarrel with a similar aged female. They are causing quite a nuisance with their foul language, as passers-by stop and stare at them. But what really catches my attention is another lady stood close by, her hands clasped to her waist and a tense look on her face. At first my observations leave me to conclude that the girl, dressed in period Victorian costume, is somehow the cause of the disturbance. I decide to walk over to the trio, but I am amazed when the girl looks up and addresses me!

"Good evening to you, Miss Brontë," she offers, with a quiet dignity, catching me completely off-guard.

"And who may you be?" I frown, somehow regaining my composure.

"Do you not recognise me, Miss Brontë? I am Sally Mitchell... a pupil at your old Sunday school."

"Bless my soul, what on earth are you doing in the midst of modern day Haworth? Is your spirit so restless that you feel the need to emerge from your tomb?"

"I am much troubled, Mistress," she said, a look of despair etching her pretty face, "You know I was with child when I reached my sixteenth year?"

"I do indeed, but was it not reported that the father of your illegitimate child was one Adam Sutherland, late of Newsholme Dene? What became of the rascal? I was led to believe he fled the area rather than answer from his crimes."

"Indeed, Mistress... but lately... before I vanquished my tenure on life, I was reliably informed my young man had been savagely beaten and his lifeless body buried on Haworth moor."

"Merciful heaven! Child, who by, pray?"

"Freda Mitchell and her two sons... My own aunt."

"Was this ever proven?"

"No, Mistress... they escaped justice because no one would come forward to testify against them."

"How did this tale come about, child?"

"My father was told it by friends of his who frequented the Black Bull. Of course, it was all hearsay with no foundation."

I frowned at the gentle-minded woman. "Pray then, why are you lingering beside this warring young couple?"

"If you please, Miss Brontë, take a close look at the young man – is it not a reincarnation of my Adam?"

After some moments of deliberation I had to agree with Miss Mitchell, but reminded her that no such thing as reincarnation had been proven – spirits of the soul, like ours, yes – but no one has ever returned to earth in a different guise or set or circumstances and been able to verify who they were. My words fell on deaf ears though; Sally was convinced that she was right and her beloved Adam was right there within arm's reach.

"Pray, what do you intend to do about the situation Miss Mitchell? You are a mere spirit like I, neither you nor I have any power over the living."

"I could rest my hand on his shoulder... maybe he will flinch at the coldness of death?" she offered, moving close to her prey as he slumped down on a park bench outside the Inn, his other lady-love now marching off into the crowd of inquisitive folk. Before I could restrain my fellow spirit, she stooped over the broken youth and placed both arms around his shoulders and she stood behind him, pressing her body up to the back of his head. As expected, there came no reaction from the weeping man and he totally ignored Miss Mitchell as he sank, with his head in his arms, over the table. Frustrated, and with a face akin to thunder, she released herself from him and resolutely sat down beside him whispering words of intimacy into his ears; yet all to no avail.

"You waste your time Miss Mitchell: we are not of this world. Arise and repair to your resting place in the church yard, I implore you."

"No, Miss Brontë, I cannot. I must make contact with my dear Adam again – for the child's sake, if not my own."

"Mercy me, why? You, your infant, Mr Sutherland... are no more. We are of the spirit world now and must forever remain so."

"I will not give up my search until Adam is once again by my side, Miss Brontë," she answered defiantly.

"Well, I fear nought will become of your mission by trying to win this present young man; he cannot see or hear you, you are unable to step over the divide of life and death, you are doomed to failure."

"No, that is not true, Miss Brontë... there is another way."

"Pray tell me child, because if there were such means of gaining the future, do you not think myself and my dear sister Emily would have used them?"

"Old Mrs Clayton, the widow of the quarry man in Marsh..."

"Martha Clayton?"

"Yes, Miss Brontë. It is common knowledge that she had a wonderful gift of thought transportation and would be willing to share it with others... at a price."

"I fear that woman was truly evil, Miss Sally, I advise you not to venture down that path. Even now, in the afterlife... she will cast a spell over you and infuriate the angels who protect us if you become friends with that woman of witchcraft!"

"It is the only way I regret to say, Miss Brontë. My child and I need Adam with us on our journey. We cannot truly enter the inner sanctum of heaven until this feat has been accomplished."

"Your mind is in turmoil, Miss Sally," I now told the gently weeping girl, "The young man you see before you is not Adam, and even if you got your wish granted, how would you transport him from his current position... brutally murder him? If you did, child, you would never enter the Kingdom of Heaven."

"Don't you see Miss Brontë? If I were afforded the gift of thought transportation I could pass over to his life and we could live happily together with my baby."

"Fiddlesticks, child!" I cried out, my patience with this headstrong young woman fast running out.

"How would he see you? He would think he was going insane, hearing voices. It would destroy him eventually – and the relationship he already owns with his real life sweetheart."

"Martha Clayton says that with the gift of telepathy comes also the gift of vision, this young man will be able to see me, to hold me and to love myself and my child as if we were alive."

"Madam! You delude yourself! This young man would cast you out into the desert of loneliness, he would have nothing to do with a spirit form - he would flee as Adam fled from your side - I am sure."

"No, Miss Brontë!" Sally cried at me in a hysterical voice fuelled by false hope and the conviction that she was right.

"You are jealous of me, Miss Brontë... just because I have the chance of happiness with a young man and you have not! I shall repair at once to seek out Martha Clayton, and then I will demonstrate to you what power I hold over life and death. I wish you good evening, Madam!"

In that moment, I believe the fire in my cheeks was hotter than all the flames in hell and damnation! The little hussy, how dare she address me so! A famous authoress and beloved daughter of Haworth! I could not avenge my fury upon her: she had gone from my presence in a white mist. I was beside myself with rage and indignation that I should be treated thus, but I realised I had no power whatsoever of preventing the Miss Sally from carrying out her threat and visiting the dubious Martha Clayton. I left the young man and stormed off up to my Parsonage home, where I spent a miserable night with my thoughts.

Sunday morning dawned bright and frosty, but I did not feel the chill that stole across the graveyard and infiltrated the silent streets of Haworth. I lay on my ghostly bed still deep in thought over my encounter with Sally Mitchell. It was folly, madness, to think that she could regain her human form and throw herself upon the mercy of that poor young man just because he bore a resemblance to her former lover. Despite the claims of Martha Clayton having the gift of sending people back from beyond the grave, I found the whole situation quite ludicrous in the extreme! To my knowledge, not one person has ever returned from the dead to inform the living what is on the other side beyond life itself, save for our dear Lord and Master, Christ Jesus. It is a fallacy to think that she, Sally Mitchell, shall be the first and forerunner of others, to rewrite history. The girl is deluded. I now remember her well from her days in my Sunday school: she was an arrogant, spiteful little child, always on the lookout for causing mischief, and the main ringleader where insolence was concerned. Many times I had complained to her parents, but their behaviour towards me was just as bad. They were indeed a rough and ready family, with both of them millworkers, and their daughter seemingly did as she pleased!

The Mitchell girl was still very much on my mind as I rose from my bed and made my way down the darkened staircase of the silent Parsonage. I glanced at the old grandfather clock that Papa religiously wound every night on his way to his bedchamber, it showed five minutes past nine. Already I could hear hushed voices coming from the direction of the offices. A new working day had begun for the staff, they were one day closer to their Christmas holidays.

I walked unseen amongst them as they drank their early morning refreshments, all chattering about what they had or had not achieved the previous night. My mind was on seeking out the whereabouts of the young man that Sally Mitchell had been yearning after. I hoped against hope that he would prove to be a mere day visitor to our humble village, and never be seen again. In that respect, Miss Mitchell would have no power of pursuing him, because like myself she was condemned to wander in close proximity to where we passed from life to death. However, the thought that Martha Clayton may intervene and change the course of history deeply troubled me. What had at first been, to me at least, a pleasant sojourn amongst the folk of Haworth and beyond, was now proving a nightmare. I felt it my duty to steer the gullible Sally Mitchell away from trouble and making herself look an imbecile in the eyes of her fellow spirits, many in number, that walked unseen amongst the living. It was a battle I must not lose!

Chapter Three

At first, all went agreeably well as I bided my time, seating myself on 'Emily's Couch' in the parlour. The historians have thus named it so because it was the place of her departure from human life, and I have no argument with the fact. It is a pity those same learned gentlemen cannot witness my dear sister now as she skips and dances joyfully over the heath beyond our former home. I know at this very moment where she will be: on the moors with Henry Moore and Annabella Shackleton, her real life friends and the inspiration - with their permission - of Heathcliff and Cathy. All three planned the story together, but it was Emily who placed it on paper.

Henry was the son of a local gypsy family, and 'Cathy' a daughter of a rich and well known family living in Buckley Green, a hamlet above Ponden. The family died out years ago and their home long demolished to make way for the man-made wonder that is Ponden Reservoir. Emily had known Annabella since early childhood, and they were one of the few families Papa let us mix with as we took our walks on the moors, passing their home in the process. However, both Papa and Annabella's parents tried to end the friendship when it was discovered we were in league with the handsome, rugged Henry. Eventually, his family moved on, but he frequently returned on his own to court his beloved... until the day they were discovered. On reflection, it would appear that my sister's friend's circumstances would run parallel with that of Sally Mitchell and her young man. Both girls became with child, out of wedlock, and both males of the union tried to flee their responsibilities. Whereas Adam Sutherland met a horrific death upon Haworth Moor, it was never proven what became of Henry after they were found together in a compromising situation. Annabella swears to this day that her father had the young gypsy murdered and his body unceremoniously buried in the soggy peat of Ponden Kirk. In normal circumstances of our time the young man would have been forced into marriage with the girl he had impregnated, but Henry's gypsy status proved too much for Annabella's family to bear, and he would never be admitted into such a respectable family. Poor Annabella was shipped out of the area forthwith to spend the rest of her days in an institution for the mentally impaired, as was the routine for girls who found themselves pregnant outside of marriage, despite their good health. A mental institution was seen as just punishment for their sins and the child would be given to a couple who were infertile. It was all very sad, but unfortunately the law of the land had to be obeyed.

Although I searched high and low, the length and breadth of Haworth throughout that Sunday, I could not locate either the young man or his real life lady-friend. So it was with some relief I settled myself inside St. Michael's Church for the 6pm carol service. By 5.30 the place was packed with folk, both from the locality and away, all chattering excitedly and ready to sing the traditional Christmastime hymns beloved by so many. No one was aware of my presence as far as I knew, but I must admit to feelings of unease when the American lady and her ageing beau walked past me; perhaps with all the crowds and chatter her powers of spirit detection would be slumbering! She passed on her way without a moment's hesitation, I am pleased to confirm.

I sat rigid for a few moments while they found a spare pew well away from me; I was so sure that this couple – or at least the lady of the party – somehow had the ability to detect me, although how and why, I knew not. It just felt so very strange, my sat amongst hundreds, and yet just one might detect and reveal my position. I hated having such troublesome thoughts as this, but I must remain always on the alert and ready to flee the church, or anywhere else for that matter, should I be unmasked. I contented myself by turning round and surveying the many faces in the church, and suddenly stiffened. There, right at the back of the building, sitting on hastily brought in small chairs, were the young man and his girlfriend, their previous argument obviously made up and forgotten about.

"Oh my dear Lord!" I cried out to myself: not three or so paces behind the pair stood Sally Mitchell, and her smile of satisfaction far surpassed the expression of the legendary Cheshire cat. I was vexed beyond the pail! I immediately rose and hurried over to my fellow spirit, her smile never leaving her face even though she had detected an angry approach.

"Miss Mitchell!" I stormed, "Is it not quite the time for you to end this nonsense and remove yourself from this holy place and the presence of this young couple?"

"I fear your request cannot be complied with Miss Brontë: I have spoken with old mother Clayton, now I own the power to do as I please!"

"Nonsense, child! I won't allow it, do you hear me? I will escort you from this church immediately!"

"Oh no you will not, Miss Brontë, you have no power or influence over me, and even if you had, I would return as soon as you went away!"

"That old witch has poisoned your mind, child: you have no power, she has tricked you into believing you are indestructible!"

"I repeat, Miss Brontë, you have no power over me!"

And she was right, I am sorry to report. Damn the child! Miss Mitchell was right in every sense of the word. As with the living, I had no intervention over the dead, I could only earnestly pray that she would do nothing to cause fear and anxiety amongst the folk present; I may as well have wished for a King's ransom! Without waiting for me to step forward, Sally Mitchell strode to the head of the church and – do not ask me how – caused the huge, golden eagle lectern to fall over, narrowly missing folks sat in the front pew opposite it. I was appalled as a great cry arose and people got up and hastily vacated their seats. The parson and several church wardens, along with a few members of the public, attempted to lift the heavy lectern back in position. On falling, it had toppled onto a pew seat and split the base asunder, wood fragments lying everywhere; had there been a person seated upon this pew they would have surely been extinguished from life in a most horrific way. As for Sally Mitchell, she rejoined me with a smug expression on her face. I was livid with her and demanded that she stopped her antics forthwith!

"In heaven's name, child! How do you think, by doing what you have just undertaken, you will gain the love and affection of the young man you so wrongly desire?"

"He is totally at my mercy, Mistress! I can, with one action, remove him from his lady love and bring him to my side like a little puppy dog!"

"And do you think he would ever dishonour himself by allowing you to dominate him? I think not, Miss Mitchell. You have created a situation that will not benefit yourself in the slightest!"

"Poppycock, madam!" she spat, taking her leave of me and sailing out of the church. I watched her departure with mounting anger and trepidation: if that young hussy now owned the power to topple heavy objects, she would surely find it a mere trifle to suddenly expose herself to the young man's vision, totally disregarding the effect that it would have on himself and his lady love. If only there was some way of warning him, indeed, of urging them to be gone from Haworth and never return. I felt so helpless and useless, unlike Miss Mitchell, I had no such power. Maybe I could seek out old Martha Clayton, and apply to her better nature to put a stop to this madness once and for all. It was my only option.

It had never been proven that Martha was a witch, just hearsay brought on by the fears of her neighbours out at Marsh, a small community to the west of Haworth at a distance of a mere half mile. She was a typical widow of our time, everyday she dressed in black as she ventured into Haworth for her groceries and other needs. Martha had owned two black cats and a fearsome Airedale terrier by the name of 'Satan'. I believe she named him thus to frighten off any strangers or inquisitive neighbours! The animal was never seen on our streets, its entire life was instead spent guarding her cottage property.

In happier times, Martha's late husband Ernest had worked up in the nearby Penistone Stone Quarry Company, earning a meagre living as a labourer. His death occurred one day while he was lifting heavy stones onto a rail truck, causing him to have a fatal heart attack. The couple had no children and so Martha was left alone in the world at a very young age. When she died of tuberculosis she was only thirty eight but carried the face and body of a very old woman. Martha was interred in the churchyard but I cannot recollect where her body was laid at the time. I had the painful task on my hands of visiting each grave of the thousands of headstones, but even then I may not find it due to the weathering effects of the last 150 years.

Chapter Four

Even though I was familiar with the surroundings, I still found myself ill at ease as I tramped through the deep carpet of frozen snow, in my quest for Martha Clayton's headstone. I had not had the misfortune of crossing her path, and hitherto prevented an unexpected encounter with one of my own kind from the realms of the undead. I certainly knew of the existence of the quarry man's wife, but my sisters and I always refrained from passing by her door. I suppose this was through an inert fear of the woman, my family and I being deeply religious. Emily set the ball rolling by laughingly suggesting the widow would fling open her front door and chase after we three sisters, reciting the Devil's cant as she did so! It was more than enough to prevent our wanderings in that direction, but like all else in life, my poor sister Emily was never taken in by the woman or her threats. Only Emily would have the nerve and questionable bravery to walk by the house! Now it was my turn to confront one of my worst nightmares, and even in death she still posed the same threat to me, or so I told myself to believe. Haworth churchyard at the dead of night was no place for the squeamish! Fortunately night or day means little to us immortals; all the same I imagined every dark tombstone had a spirit hiding behind it, ready to pounce! It was an irrational fear borne of contempt of the woman who laughed in the face of religion and my Lord. It was good against evil as far as I was concerned: Martha Clayton had to be dealt with and her new apprentice humbled.

I searched for a good hour but no sign did I find of the grave; what I needed to do was search the church burial plans, but they were locked away in the archives in Keighley and consequently well out of the area my spirit form was permitted to wander.

***

Next morning, Haworth was totally deserted of the weekend's visitors. Not even by eleven o'clock did I espy more than a dozen of people walking about forlornly in a grey mist, blotting out the snowy roofs of the village. Nearby, a steam train hoot rented the stillness, but there would be few takers that day for the carriage ride to Oxenhope or Keighley. I had the streets to myself, and with it the comforting thought that the young couple had returned home well out of reach of the scheming Miss Mitchell! Yet, I was not utterly alone with my thoughts, more's the pity! A few minutes into my silent patrol of Main Street I was joined by another, less desirable, personage in the shape of the aforementioned Sally Mitchell and she seemed far from convivial! I became aware of her presence as I peered into the darkened display window of 'Spooks', the little shop selling all sorts to do with the supernatural and the afterlife.

"I find it most comforting, Miss Brontë, that you show interest in such a frowned-upon business by you religious people!" a familiar voice suddenly echoed in my ears.

"Good morning to you, Miss Mitchell. I trust you have seen the error of your ways now the young man has vacated our rude streets for his home?"

"Nonsense, Miss Brontë," sneered my spectral companion, folding her arms and giving me an indignant glance before turning to point out a building on the opposite side of the street.

"Yonder building is where my young man resides with his despicable lady-friend; they are not yet gone from Haworth as you so keenly hoped, Miss Brontë!"

"How do you know all this?" I demanded, a feeling of cold fear rushing through my soul.

"I saw them repair there late last evening and they have not yet emerged. I have kept the place under close observation all through the night."

So it seemed my worst fears were founded: this little vixen was determined to ruin the lives of the two young innocents, by her ruthlessly demanding ways, to get what she wanted. I was now certain that Miss Mitchell was a daughter of Satan, and was to be vanquished at all costs. But what could I do on my own? No spirit force of my existence could stop this mad young woman, it needed the efforts of a human, preferably a member of the clergy who dealt in exorcism. But where does one find such an individual in Haworth? I knew of no-one in my time, and I certainly did not know the whereabouts of one in modern life. If I were lucky enough to stumble across such a divine person, how would I communicate my fears to him about Miss Mitchell? Or should I, on some pretence, visit Martha Clayton and plead for some unknown power to myself so that I might fight

Miss Mitchell on even terms? This whole scenario seemed ludicrous: two spirits quarrelling over a human being, breathing and living their life happily in their own time and world! Perhaps my sister Emily could offer some advice?

"What are you thinking, Miss Brontë?" came a quiet voice to my mind.

"I am thinking that you are a disgrace to your kind, Miss Mitchell! We are from beyond the grave and populating a different dimension to these folk living on earth. We should console ourselves with the thought that we lived our lives to the expectations of our Lord, and be gracious in our thanks to Him. We have no authority over the living and no matter what magical powers that Clayton woman has seemingly bestowed upon you, will ever bring you happiness. We have had our lives Miss Mitchell, now let them enjoy theirs. Our two worlds must never join, it is not permitted by God: no one, save for His dear Son, may step over the threshold from death to life, whatever the urgent circumstances."

"If you have quite finished furnishing me with useless thoughts, Miss Brontë, may I suggest you wander off and leave me to dispense with my own pleasures?"

"Hah! You call this a pleasure? Hounding an innocent young man wherever he goes, just because you falsely determine that he is a replica of your lost Adam? You are a fool, Miss Mitchell. Can you not see that no power, good or evil, will allow you to come back to the land of the living? We are spirits and will ever remain so until our Lord's second coming!"

"You delude yourself, Miss Brontë," my companion sneered, "do you not see the wonderful opportunity we have here? Not only can we walk amongst the living, but also become one of them!"

"And, pray, where will you live when you are not chasing the young man? What about your clothes, work, family?"

"Do not concern yourself with my welfare, Miss Brontë. Given the power I will be able to enjoy both worlds, spiritual and living."

"If what you say is true, how may I share in your good fortune then?" I asked with bated breath: I had a cunning plan! However, Sally Mitchell was suspicious of me and would not give in to my polite question.

"Why would you need to go into modern life, Miss Brontë? All whom you ever knew passed away peacefully."

"I would love the chance to become part of the modern society – under a non-deplume of course – I would certainly enjoy myself in a modern world."

"And take to your side a new gentleman, perhaps?"

"Indeed, Miss. Mitchell, I find that thought most agreeable!"

"Would you travel beyond our village though, Belgium perchance?"

"Belgium? No! I fear that country holds too many painful memories for me... no, I would never be so foolhardy or headstrong, in the way of my youth."

"It is common knowledge that you were deeply in love with M'sieur Heger?"

I winced: the confounded girl! She had sought and found a tender nerve, still raw despite the passage of many years since that tragic event that brought upon me such misery and heartache. And for what gain? None. My darling Constantin turned his face from me, casting me aside like any other worthless schoolgirl. I loved and lost, yet I never gained his love in the first instance. I looked at Miss Mitchell, it would appear that she was enjoying my discomfort. I decided to relieve myself of her company and made my way back up Main Street after making a feeble excuse.

I did not venture out further that day but contented myself watching the comings and goings of the staff and the dismal attendance of a few visitors to the Parsonage. Miss Mitchell did not bother me again that day; indeed my old home was out of bounds to her wandering spirit, just as I were to her former dwelling on Changegate during the last few days of her life. Her parents had just relinquished their other home as Sally was taken ill. By the by, I had no sympathy for the child either in life or death: she was always seeking out ways of making people's lives a misery with her unruly behaviour.

Chapter Five

The following day there was very few staff in evidence during the hour of luncheon, so I took it upon myself to venture into the old library and peruse a few of the hundreds of old books securely locked away in the huge glass cabinet - but not secure enough for my spirit fingers – my spiritual hands knew no human obstacle and I could do as I pleased. I was thus engrossed that I failed to see a grey figure enter by the old, bricked up doorway and come over to me.

"Miss Brontë?"

I whirled round and came face to face with a smartly dressed young man, one whom I immediately recognised as being Mr Adam Sutherland!

"Bless my soul!" I cried out, my right hand patting my chest as I stepped back a pace, "You startled me Sir!"

"I do beg your pardon, Miss Brontë," he smiled, removing his top hat and bowing gracefully before me.

"What brings you into my domain, Mr Sutherland?" I smiled wanly.

"I am searching for my Sally, have you seen her of late?"

"I must confess this is the case... very recently in fact!"

"You appear a little tense, Miss Brontë. Have you exchanged heated words?"

"Indeed so, Sir, I fear you are most correct."

"And what terrible thing has she managed to do this time?" he smiled, placing himself on a swivel chair next to what you modern day folk would call a computer.

"She has sought out old Mrs Clayton and obtained some sort of power from her... the power, so she would have us believe, to step from death to life and live in the modern world!"

"Fantasy, my dear lady!" Mr Sutherland cried, his face bursting into merriment, "I have never heard such poppycock!"

"Do beg me forgiveness for asking, Mr Sutherland, but have you not previously entertained the notion to search out Miss Mitchell? Why, it must be upwards of 150 years that have passed by since your demise!"

"Surely I have, Miss Brontë, but each time I seem to be thwarted in my endeavours, I do not believe our Lord wishes Miss Mitchell and I to meet in reconciliation."

"Perhaps you are right Sir, it is not for you and I to judge the intentions of our Maker, but I find it rather sad in the extreme that you are not allowed to look upon the face of your child and its mother. Miss Mitchell informs me that you were murdered on, or very near, Haworth moor by three of her relatives... is that the case Sir? If you would not mind my interference on the subject."

"Yes, it is true, Miss Brontë: I was indeed disposed of in a most gruesome way and my earthly remains buried in a shallow grave on the moor."

"Can you remember where, Sir?"

"Why the interest Miss Brontë? Are you hoping to put Miss Sally's mind at rest by discovering my body?"

"No Sir, that is not the case. I was more concerned that you should have a proper Christian burial in the new cemetery. It is not right that you should remain lost and forgotten."

"I do not understand your plan, Miss Brontë. How will you alert my whereabouts to the proper authorities? You are a mere spirit blessed with no such powers."

"Neither is your Miss Mitchell, Sir, but she feels confident that she will regain life as a young woman again, with the help of the Clayton woman."

"For what purpose, pray?" frowned Mr Sutherland.

"There is a young man residing in our village at this hour, he is a mere visitor and will be gone shortly, but your Miss Mitchell has convinced herself that you are he, reincarnated."

"Upon my soul, Miss Brontë! You jest with me, do you not?" cried Mr Sutherland, quickly rising from his chair.

"No, Sir, I speak the truth: Miss Mitchell fully intends to enter the realm of the living again, and chase after this young man... even though a lady-friend already shares his company."

"It cannot be done, Madam!" cried Mr Sutherland, smacking a fist into the palm of his other hand, his face now a mask of indignation at the thought of his former lover having romantic pretensions for a human. I steeled myself, I could sense a drama unfolding, and with the innocent young man at the centre of this love triangle. I tried to calm Mr Sutherland down by suggesting that our Lord would never allow a spirit access to the modern world, magical powers or no. Thankfully he accepted my suggestion and slumped back into the seat.

"We must put a stop to this madness, Miss Brontë," he said.

Just at that point, two ladies entered the library, and the taller one promptly sat on the chair occupied by Mr Sutherland, and just as promptly vacated it!

"Gemma? What's wrong... have you sat on a pin or something?" laughed her shorter companion.

"No I haven't, but there is something weird going on!"

"Weird?"

"Yes, this chair is freezing cold... you feel!"

"Oh! So it is... but the heating's on in here? I don't understand... and there are no windows open?"

"Maybe we should fetch Andrew?"

"And tell him what?"

"Well I don't know... Oh, give me a cushion off the lounge chair. I'll sit on that."

Her order duly carried out, the irate young woman again sat down on the invisible knees of Mr Sutherland, much to his merriment. I watched disgustedly as his hands went round her waist and then ventured up to the woman's ample bosom; I hurried from the room for decency's sake! That Mr Sutherland was a lecher of the worst kind. Thanks heavens the librarian was not aware of his fingers caressing her most intimate places! I dreaded to think where they would go next as he espied her bare legs protruding from her extremely short skirt!

My hurried departure was immediately arrested as I almost collided with a person knocking on the library door. As she was summoned in by one of the staff I realised it was the American woman again! My vexation of Mr Sutherland was immediately replaced by mild curiosity at this woman's intrusion of the library, which is out of bounds to most of the general public, unless one has received a formal invitation. So I rejoined the group, totally ignoring Mr Sutherland. The girl who had been sitting innocently on his lap had got to her feet to shake hands with the American woman and ask how she could be of assistance.

"Is this place haunted by the Brontë family, honey? I'd kinda like to research it for a book I'm currently writing on English ghosts."

"You couldn't have chosen a better time!" laughed the taller girl, but was immediately snubbed by her shorter companion as owning too wild an imagination!

"Gemma sat on that chair and complained it felt icy cold, odd considering how warm the library is."

"Hmm?" said the American lady, briefly bending to examine the swivel chair, "Kinda like it could be the material it's made from, I guess."

"So what makes you think the Parsonage is haunted then?" asked Leonie, the shorter female.

"Well I know for sure Haworth Main Street is... I had an experience the other day, I felt someone was following me. And now, in this room, I feel there is a person, or persons, watching us as we speak!"

"How awfully interesting," mused Gemma, motioning their guest into a spare seat, "Tell me, do you deal in psychocism as a hobby?"

"I do indeed, Ma'am. I can instantly pick up on spirits if they are around, like now," she turned to face me, "See in that corner, by the filing cabinet, I can detect something really strong!"

"Man or woman would you say?"

"Difficult to tell, honey, but my guess is it's a woman... maybe the wife of that Reverend Wade guy who built this extension the library sits on? Remember, this would have been their living quarters."

I sighed with relief, at least the meddlesome woman had no idea she was face to face with Charlotte Brontë! I looked round at Mr Sutherland, but he had gone! The situation must have unnerved him and he'd left. I decided to test the American woman and moved closer, but to my horror and consternation, my long trailing dress swished by some papers and caused them to flutter to the carpet in an untidy pile!

"See that!" cried the American woman, springing to her feet, "How'd you explain that? There are no windows or doors open! No draught could have done that!"

I stood there mortified! How could such a thing have befallen me? I had no magical powers. I was at the mercy of the people in the room now. I need not have concerned myself though: they, as one, fled. I remained motionless, trying desperately to find an explanation for this sudden occurrence that rendered me almost human. The people in the room had not given the impression that I could be seen, merely heard. They had jolted themselves into puzzlement as to what could have caused the papers to spread themselves into an untidy collection on the carpet. My first thought was that, somehow, Miss Mitchell had a hand in this: But how? She was nowhere in evidence. Maybe, then, it was the work of Martha Clayton. I looked around the now silent room, only the flickering of the computer screen broke the spell of isolation: I needed to leave before something dreadful befell me.

I was very cross with myself as I stood in the garden looking at the main entrance to my former home. What on earth did I need to concern myself with? Perhaps it was a mere fluke that the documents fell, maybe the pile had not been evenly stacked? The folk brushing past me as they paid to go into the museum certainly had no idea I was stood only a short distance away watching their movements. Eventually, I saw the American lady speedily pass by the entrance gate of our garden and flee into the relative safety of the village. I decided not to follow her hasty retreat, enough consternation had been shared out for the moment. Instead, I decided to seek out Miss Mitchell.

My mission proved easier than expected: I found the young, troublesome female in the usual haunt, outside the Black Bull.

"Miss Mitchell!" I screeched, making her jump, "What is the meaning of this... causing me to deliberately drop important papers onto the library carpet in full view of humans?"

"Pray, I have no idea what you are talking about Miss Brontë: I have never ventured anywhere near your old home, let alone inside it!" retaliated my irate companion, her face looking cold and sullen.

"Well I do declare I had not the power to remove objects hitherto this day!"

"It was either a coincidence or you are trying to make an issue out of it to suit your own ends."

"I totally deny that Miss Mitchell... what use would I have for owning magical powers?"

"Forgive me, Miss Brontë, but were you not, just a short while ago, exploring the possibility of visiting my good friend Martha? I believe you said that you wanted to gain magical powers from her so that you may pleasingly transport yourself forwards in time?"

"This I may have said, but I certainly was not aware that I already owned strange powers!"

"Oh, just forget it, Miss Brontë... the falling papers... no one saw you as a person, did they not?"

"No, indeed, but the falling of the papers caused them much excitement and fear."

"A natural reaction, I daresay, Miss Brontë?"

"The implications are too serious to ignore, child!" I rounded on my grinning companion.

"Oh, do calm yourself Miss Brontë. No one beheld you, for all they know it could have been caused by any number of spirits. Let them speculate if they must but they will never agree on a right answer."

"Are you sure you have not been deceitful with me in this delicate matter, Miss Mitchell?"

"In what respect, pray?"

"Have you approached Martha Clayton and requested her to place some sort of mischievous spell upon my poor person?"

"Indeed, I have not, Miss Brontë! Why would I take great comfort in watching you struggle with the unknown? I have only approached Martha to suit my own needs, and that is only to reveal myself to the young man."

"I beg to inform you Miss Mitchell, you need not have wasted your time on such a request, and it may interest you to know that I have been speaking with your Mr Sutherland quite recently."

"What! Where?" shrieked Miss Mitchell, walking right up to face me.

"In the Parsonage, Miss Mitchell... he was searching for you."

"I do not understand... How can he when his grave lies over at Newsholme Dene? We spirits are prisoners of our own surroundings; we are never allowed to stray far from the place where we departed this life."

"I beg leave to differ with you, Miss Mitchell. Is it not a fact that my dear sister Emily takes regular sojourns upon the moors and yet she did not die upon the heath-land."

"I agree that is so, Miss Brontë, but I myself am allowed no passage further than the village limits, and you, dear lady, what is the extent of your wanderings?"

"I cannot truthfully tell you Miss Mitchell, I have neither felt the need nor inclination to stray far from my home or the village centre. If I were suddenly possessed with the urgency for adventure maybe I would choose to go with Emily on her moor walks, if the Lord allowed me that privilege."

"I daresay he would, Miss Brontë, you have done no wrong to warrant total confinement to Haworth."

"And you have, I take it?"

"Indeed so, I fear: in life I took every opportunity with the men of Haworth, even those that were married. I lived my life as I chose even though, for decency's sake, I never admitted to my parents or relatives that I was a fallen woman."

"Miss Mitchell!" I cried out in disgust, "Shall I assume you are telling me you procured the men folk of this village for sexual misdoings... a street-madam?"

"Yes, Miss Brontë. My family were very poor and the extra money proved an admirable bounty to help with our needs."

"Upon my soul, child, how did you explain your sudden good fortune to your destitute parents?"

"I informed them that I have taken a part time position in a local hostelry in Keighley... my father, as you know, suffered badly from a deformed leg and so he was not able to visit my place of work, nor could he afford a coach fare."

"But surely, the men of Haworth whom you entertained would loosen their tongues over pints of ale in the Black Bull, or wherever? You were treading a dangerous path, Miss Mitchell. What I find most abhorrent is the thought of men abusing your body. It is most disgusting!" I said, taking up my long dress and storming off, "I bid you a good day!"

Miss Mitchell shouted after me, telling me that had I been poor, I would have done the same... the wretched child!

Chapter Six

A few days after the incident with Miss Mitchell, and being no nearer apprehending that vile creature Martha Clayton, I noticed that a Christmas play was to be performed in my old school rooms opposite the Parsonage. I refer, of course, to the low building known as the Sunday school which had been built with help from my own funds. The play was to be held on Christmas Eve itself, so I decided I would secretly attend in order to view the players and how good their acting was! The notice board indicated that the local theatre company were putting on a performance about a Victorian family Christmas. No doubt it would be more lavish than anything our family used to know!

By the time I entered the building the hall was packed with folk all chattering away, like a room of caged birds, prior to the play starting. I stole to the back of the hall and was suddenly made aware of the presence of Martha Clayton and her protégé Sally Mitchell! I was about to hasten away when they themselves fled before me, the old hag cheerfully raising her hand in greeting to me. I was appalled and wanted nothing to do with the pair of them, though I keenly watched their departure.

Suddenly they stopped and turned to look my way. Martha raising her right arm and pointing at me, I saw her lips move briefly until she collapsed with laughter. Martha and Miss Mitchell both disappeared from my sight.

"Well!" I cried, anger rising up in my throat as I moved close to the rear of the hall and positioned myself on a vacant chair next to an attractive young gentleman. I settled myself for an enjoyable evening, but moments later my spirit world fell apart when the dark haired fellow turned to address me.

"Shouldn't you be up on stage with the rest of the cast?" he smiled.

I sat there rigid with shock. Were I not a spirit from the realms of the undead, were I not invisible to all?

"Upon my soul... you can see me?" I blurted forth, holding a gloved hand over my mouth.

"Of course I can! Why, did you think I was drunk or something?" he laughed, fixing his ice blue eyes upon myself. I must admit I felt quite arrested by his goodness and handsome features, but I was in dire straits:

how on earth could this gentleman see me, unless he had magical powers? My thoughts turned to Martha Clayton. She must have cast a spell over me! There seemed no other explanation. Now what could be done to escape this madness?

"I like your clothes, you look really authentic" smiled my companion, displaying two rows of perfectly white teeth, "What's your name?"

"I – I – I am called Charlotte, Sir... please forgive my ragged speech, but you took me quite unawares for a moment there."

"Did I? Why?"

"It is nothing," I answered dismissively.

"I'm Mike," he grinned and held his hand forward to shake. Now I really did feel the icy fingers of doom stealing down my spine as I reluctantly held forth my own hand, expecting a loud cry as his fingers closed over fresh air. I closed my eyes, steeling myself for the inevitable. But it never came; I felt his warm grasp, he mine. Satisfied, he withdrew his hand and once again remarked that I should be making a move for the stage, as the performance was about to begin.

"I am not in the play. I am merely here to watch, the same as you."

"Why wear the traditional Victorian dress then? Do you work in one of the shops?"

"No Sir, I certainly do not!" I cried, "I'll have you know that I am an accomplished writer of modern romance."

"Really? Well this is my lucky day, meeting a real life lady novelist. Tell me, where do you get your ideas from?"

"The study of local villagers, mostly" I answered proudly.

"Have you had anything published?"

"Indeed I have, several in fact!"

"Have you? What name do you go under? Or do you use your own?"

"I once used a pseudonym, but now I have reverted back to my proper name. There was no point in the deception Sir, when everyone knew me in Haworth anyway."

"No need to keep calling me 'Sir'!" he grinned, his eyes twinkling.

"What – may I be so bold to enquire – is your nature of work?"

"I'm a cop."

"A what?" I frowned, feeling my face becoming uncomfortably warm.

"I'm a police officer. I drive the squad car," he explained, giving me a rather odd look.

"Oh, so I am in safe hands then?" I managed to smile.

"You're a strange one, Charlotte... I think you're taking the mick a bit here."

"I beg your pardon?"

"Forget it," he shrugged, displaying yet another broad grin. I reciprocated but my mind was in utter turmoil. I needed to make my escape from this sudden nightmare situation I found myself in. But the young man was so pleasant and agreeable that in spite of my nervousness I felt it would be greatly rude of me to excuse myself. I fear I rather liked him!

Nothing more was said between us because the play had begun: it was quite admirable, but I thought the cast rather overdid things, portraying a Victorian family Christmas which was far removed from my own experiences. I suppose the exaggerations were to please the audience, but I can confirm that many of the things enacted – like after tea games – were not even invented during my lifetime. Nor were some of the Christmas carols sung by the cast! The performance ended within an hour to enthusiastic applause. I was about to turn to my companion in order to ask his opinion, but we were interrupted by a pleasant looking young lady.

"Hi Claire," smiled Mike. He gestured towards me, "This is Charlotte, we met earlier this evening, she writes romantic novels."

"Really?" smiled Claire, introducing herself as Mike's younger sister. "I like the clothes Charlotte, you look great!"

"Thank you," I smiled, giving a neat little bow of my head.

"So are you a member of the cast?"

"Unfortunately not, I am merely a spectator like your dear brother."

"Dear brother? That's a laugh!" erupted Claire, playfully pushing Mike.

"So what line of work are you in when you're not writing?"

"Writing is my work, though I do spend some of my time wandering around my locality."

"How boring!"

"I do not find it so," I retaliated a little coldly.

"Now then, sis, each to their own," warned Mike. Claire looked keenly at me, and then at my attire, her interest excited by my choice of dress.

"Why have you come to the play dressed similarly to the cast?" she asked abruptly, folding her arms; I had to think quickly!

"It is all in spirit of the festive season," I smiled nervously, but she appeared satisfied with my explanation.

"Has Mike offered to take you for a drink after the show?"

"No, but I am afraid I would have to decline his generous offer. I do not partake of intoxicating beverages."

"Very sensible," smiled Mike, "what sort of car do you drive, Charlotte?"

"I am afraid that I own no such conveyance. I go where I will on foot."

"What? And you're a published writer? I find that hard to believe! You could afford a Rolls on your salary I bet?"

"Sorry?" I frowned.

"A Rolls Royce, you know, a big swanky car?"

"I fear you have confused me there, Sir. I am unsure of what you are referring to?"

Both brother and sister looked at each other, Claire frowning and whispering something in his ear, making him smile. I felt my cheeks burning, they had gained much entertainment from my last sentence. If only I could escape this terrible situation I had found myself in. Claire then returned to my side, arms folded and a cruel smile on her fresh young face.

"I can see it all now," she said, briefly turning to look at her grinning brother, "You are playing some sort of charade, making out that you are the image of Charlotte Brontë: am I right?"

I looked from one to the other: this was total madness!

"My name really is Charlotte and I am a novelist! That is all you need to know from me, Madam!"

"Madam?!" cried Claire, her eyes darting into mine as she stood over me menacingly, "You have a nerve calling me that! I suppose you think you're special, dressing up in some costume and writing slushy stories!"

"If you will please excuse me, I fear it is time I relinquished myself from your company. I bid you both good evening!" I said, gaining my feet and giving a polite bow to them.

"Hang about Charlotte, I'll walk you home," offered Mike.

"No need Sir, I can find my own way."

"Maybe you can, but the streets are no place for a young woman on her own at night."

"Very well," I sighed, dismay etching my mind. Where could I walk him to before slipping silently into the darkness? Being an officer of the law, I knew he would keep a keen and diligent observation over me. Damn that Martha Clayton and her cohort Mitchell, they were responsible for my plight!

Chapter Seven

It is fair to say that I walked that night in a state of excited fear and suspense: my handsome escort politely by my side, his hands dutifully behind his back for the most part, the poor man totally unaware to whom he was offering protection. I was indeed grateful that he did not try to seek my hand or place a protective arm around my shoulder; I would indeed have died, if that were ever possible, dear Reader!

Here I was, a daughter of a once famous parson, alone on a darkened street with a total stranger. It assured me not that he was a man of the law; he was a man with thoughts and aspirations, after all. I am still quite shaken that the poor creature offered me so much of his attention when there were so many other more attractive ladies in evidence that evening, all milling around and chatting after the play had concluded. Perhaps I stood out from the crowd with my plainness, small stature and clothes that were far from elegant! Maybe he found me more interesting and mysterious? Whatever his pretensions, I was desperate to leave his side and return to my own world, I felt naked and vulnerable in this modern setting.

When I began this narrative to you, the Reader, I was a contented spirit, unseen and unheard, living in my own world beyond the grave. Now look at me! Thrust through time by some scheming old hag, to sustain quiet revenge on me for insulting her young follower. I reasoned that there was no escape for me, I was powerless to remove myself to my own world without the help of the one who sent me there. I felt wretched and frightened by my ordeal as I walked with my arms folded, down the steepness of Main Street, ignoring the shouts and noise of young partygoers on their way to the Inns for a night of drunken debauchery. I was trapped with no way out, what had I done to deserve this terrible catastrophe?

"You're very quiet Charlotte, are you ok?" a manly voice broke into my thoughts. It was caring of Mike, of course, but I could not accept his words of warmth; all I longed for was escape from this awful dilemma.

"Have we far to go?" he continued, briefly touching my upper arm and gently pulling my black cloak further over my quaking body. "You're shivering," he said.

"No, not much further now," I managed, "I beg you leave me as we enter Sun Street... my father... he is very protective of me."

"Sure, if that's what you want. But may I see you again sometime?"

I looked at Mike briefly and then carried on walking with my head bowed down.

"There were many other ladies at the play who were much nicer than me, I am quite plain!"

"Rubbish, Charlotte! I don't think you are," he smiled, his strong arm snaking behind my bonnet and gripping my shoulder! I found myself frozen indeed with fear as he gently pulled me towards him.

"Mike!" I squealed, pushing him away as he tried to kiss me.

"I'm sorry," he said, releasing me, "I didn't mean to frighten you."

"I accept your apology, but please do not presume on me further, Sir!"

"There you go again, calling me 'Sir'. What is it with you girl?"

"You will have to forgive me, it is the way I was brought up, I am obliged by decency to call all gentlemen by that title." "Well you can stop calling me it, I hate it!" he cried.

Suddenly, to my profound relief, there came a deep silence between us as we reached the bottom of Main Street and crossed the busy road by the old chapel at Bridgehouse Lane. I eventually broke the stillness.

"Where is your home, Mike?"

"Lodge Lane, in Keighley," came the dull response. I looked at him, and seeing the hurt in his eyes, offered my hand to his face.

Yet, dear Reader, in that moment of tenderness my ordeal was over; I hastened back to my own world without my knowledge! I became aware that something was terribly amiss when Mike frantically began to call out my name, a demonic look entering his eyes. I was awfully afraid of him until common sense told me that I was no longer at the centre of his vision. Somehow or other, Martha Clayton's strangulated grip on me had been torn asunder by a much higher authority, and I had gained my invisibility once more. In that moment of realisation, I keenly felt the excitement of relief, but this was coupled with the sadness for poor Mike: he was jerking wildly about in the darkness, trying unsuccessfully to find me. Suddenly, as if by magic, he froze, his eyes taking on the glazed look of deep shock. I felt so sorry for my handsome young gentleman and longed to hold him, but my earthly body was no longer in existence. Long moments passed in which I knew it would be folly to try and offer help to the astounded soul. I was now where I should have been, I was a free spirit, the shackles of earth had fallen from me; once again, I became a servant of death.

***

All through that long winter's night, lying in my secret bedchamber, my thoughts were on my handsome escort and my sudden disappearance from his side. I tried to imagine how I would feel if I had been on the receiving end of this phenomenon, had he been in the spirit world and I a living being. Poor man, I felt drawn to him as a mother is drawn to her whimpering child; nay, more than that, I experienced something far stronger than a mother's love, something I had felt only in the distant past when Constantin Heger occupied my every waking moment for months on end. But surely not? This is madness, I hardly knew Mike, and there was always his ill-tempered sister Claire to consider. And yet he had somehow unlocked my aching heart and allowed all my womanly feelings to rush forth like a mighty tidal wave! I checked myself, I sternly rebuked such nonsensical thoughts, my long years of death had poisoned my soul. It is not love that I felt for that young officer of the law, just fantasy borne of depression for something I never possessed in real life. And then it hit me with such force that it caused me to jolt upright in my bed: Mike was the image of Constantin Heger, complete with small black beard! Oh, Heaven help me! Dear Lord, now I can understand how Sally Mitchell first felt when she came upon the young man outside the Black Bull. This is pure madness, the work of that Clayton witch! On the morrow, I determined to confront the old hag and render her incapable of ever hurting me again, by whatever foul means possible.

Chapter Eight

By this time it was Christmas Day, and I had the Parsonage to myself. I believed that there was no one around to detect my movements, apart from the discreetly placed security cameras of course, but they scarcely mattered. The hour was early, barely eight in the morning, when I had risen with my resolve stronger than ever. I was determined to confront Martha Clayton for all the hurt she had brought upon myself and Sally Mitchell. Somehow or other my Waterloo was fast approaching; I earnestly prayed for my Lord's help as I sank to my knees in front of the parlour couch on which my poor sister Emily departed from life. I knew not whether my prayers had been answered as I ventured outside into the deep snow. It had fallen heavily during the night and drifts piled themselves up the front door and to the very sills of the lower windows. The white landscape proved no obstacle for my spirit form, I merely glided through it as I reached the lane beyond the garden gate. I proceeded in the direction of the church which stood ominously dark against the brilliance of the snow. I paused briefly by the cemetery gate, there was no point in my searching for Martha's grave in those conditions, and I determined to walk the mile or so to her old cottage at Marsh. I am sure she could be found haunting the home she passed away in, and I also hoped Miss Mitchell would be present too!

Main Street was bereft of people on this snowy morn, only a solitary robin called out briefly as it alighted on top of a boundary wall. I slowly passed by, reaching out to pat the little birds head, he was of course unaware of my ghostly being trying to interrupt his beautiful morning song! As I did so I glanced up at the building Miss Mitchell had pointed out to me and I wondered whether the young man and his girl were still there. It seemed hardly possible now that Christmas was upon us; they would be long gone from our streets, happily seeking warmth and shelter somewhere beyond Haworth.

My thoughts turned to the previous evening when I had similarly reached out thus, seeking not a little bird's head, but rather the warm face of a man who had tugged at my heartstrings, a man I knew I could no longer burden with my presence. The evil power that had held me in its grip was now no more, I was once again free to roam where I pleased; and yet, I felt the loss of my handsome escort most keenly. In my day, gentlemen who had arrested my attention had been few and far between, my plain features ensured a barrier between myself and the opposite sex. The few suitors I had were nondescript, only asking for my hand in marriage as a mark of selfish decency. My eventual husband, Arthur Bell Nicholls, was at once different to the others, but he did not excite the feelings that I had recently experienced in the presence of that modern day policeman! Our mode of courting had been vastly different, and in my time decency was the watchword of all. Mike had openly chatted to me without asking any permission, but I do confess that I felt flattered by his attentions for such a 'Plain Jane' as myself! He saw beyond my poor looks and discovered something more to his liking, I suspect.

I laughed to myself as I slowly walked along, not making a single footprint in the soft snow to mark my passing. To Mike, I was yet another female to chat to, and a very nervous one at that! But where could it all lead? I was of the spirit world, there was no chance of a union between us, and now poor Mike would realise for himself that I was a product of the world beyond earth. My demonstration of invisibility had rendered him to a frozen imbecile, I do declare I have never seen such a mortal reduced to a granite statue! What had marked a return to normality for my spirit self, must have seemed to Mike a nightmare. How miserable I felt for him at that moment, but there was nothing I could do.

In life, my circumstances were much complicated, but now, even in death, they seemed doubly compounded! In my lifetime I tried to imagine what things would be like 'on the other side': now I knew! Passion for someone you could never have was just as brutal and heartbreaking in death as in life. Before death I was a woman yearning to be loved for who I was, not just as the author of Jane Eyre... outwardly I was an ordinary human being in need of love and comfort, it was only my active mind which aroused excitement in the general public. I rather think, though, that my sister Emily was the only one of we three sisters to encounter deep passion out there on her beloved moors, though with whom, I did not know. Although as sisters we never withheld secrets from each other, I firmly believe to this day that my fiery sister was enjoying a deep relationship with a mystery man – maybe one of the many hill farmers, maybe someone from the nearby stone quarries – although no one has ever come forward to admit any indiscretions with Emily. It is perhaps possible that this person was already wedded to a local girl and was enjoying extra connivances with my rebel sister. Emily was indeed a bad apple when it came to acting prim and proper; it would not surprise me in the slightest if there was a man in her life. Where else could she have got her material to create Heathcliff and Cathy? I know that her two friends were helping her, through relating their own experiences, but I suspect there was a fourth person involved: Emily's lover!

By the by, all this speculation was not helping my own situation; I was deeply embroiled with something I had no control over. In one respect Martha Clayton had brought me Mike, but realistically she was only goading me into doing something that clashed with my religious beliefs, trying to make me think there may be power away from our Lord. I was very surprised that my guardian angel had not stepped in to put an end to this nonsense; obviously my Lord above was willing to tolerate the situation a little longer before bringing an end to my hopeless dilemma. Maybe I was being shown the happiness that had been lacking in my former life? I surprised myself in finding how easy and comfortable I felt when I spoke with Mike or was in his company. I had always been a very sickly person, prone to severe headaches if I had to entertain society, and I would often shrink away into my shell. With Mike it felt pleasantly different, and my normally red cheeks did not suffer under the heat of embarrassment or shyness, at least when Claire refrained from asking confusing questions. However, whether I liked him or not, I knew that this present situation must not be permitted to continue under any circumstances. Severance from Mike and the living world was inevitable, and in my spirit life I could return to what I loved doing best: walking unseen amongst the tourists and good folk of present day Haworth. I really must find Martha Clayton!

Sadly, in this endeavour I did not succeed although I walked for miles that morning, calling out her name in the vicinity of her old home. I had convinced myself that she would be present in order to keep a close eye on the comings and goings of her former abode. I even ventured within, under the very noses of the present owners, but no trace could I find of the evasive old troublemaker. I could have called her 'witch' to you, the

Reader, but even after a gap of over a hundred and fifty years I still did not know whether she was a true sister of the Coven: it was all hearsay in my time, and no substantial proof had ever been gained to prove such accusations. Yet in my present situation, I was inclined to think the rumours were true. Whatever old Martha had said to me the evening of the play had rendered me defenceless against her power. Thank God it was only of a temporary nature!

I made my way back to Haworth along Sun Street, after more fruitless searching, intending to return home to the Parsonage. I knew my sister Emily would not be far away; she loved to wander our old home at Christmastime and reflect on her youth, recalling the days when we all crowded into the kitchen to watch old Tabby Ackroyd make platefuls of delicious mince pies! I was thus engrossed with my happy thoughts that I failed to notice the misty form of Sally Mitchell walking alongside me to bid good morning.

"You!" I choked, quite startled by her sudden presence.

"Good morning to you too," she smiled, "and, pray, where have you been sojourning this beautiful winter's day?"

"As if you did not know!" I replied curtly, never faltering or slowing my step.

"Really, Miss Brontë!" she cried indignantly, going on to assure me that she did not follow me everywhere I went.

"If that is the case, Miss Mitchell, then I apologise. But, perhaps, if I appeal to your better nature you may furnish me with some intelligence?"

"About what, pray?"

"Your friend Martha Clayton?"

"And what, pray, do you require of me concerning that dear creature?"

"I would hardly describe her thus, Miss Mitchell, Martha has been instrumental in bringing me much sorrow of late."

"In what respect, Miss Brontë?" frowned Sally.

"She placed a spell on me, did she not, at the performance at my old Sunday school?"

"Perhaps, but no harm was occasioned to your person I hope?"

"No harm? I beg leave to disagree Miss Mitchell, very much harm has been procured by the whims of your mystic friend!"

Sally frowned at me as we came to a brief halt.

"Yes, you may look concerned," I told her, biting my lip, "A young, living, man has taken it upon himself to honour me with his presence, and seeks further acquaintance with me."

Sally Mitchell's jaw sagged open.

"Oh, good Lord! You mean to say... Martha really can cross the barriers of time? The young man could actually see and speak with you?"

"You seem surprised Miss Mitchell, has this happened to you also with your young man?"

"Most certainly not, Miss Brontë!" she cried out, her face looking flushed and angry in thinking I had gained a victory over her.

"Your Martha Clayton appears to be choosy in evincing the gift of life."

"Wait while I see her, the wretch!" cried Sally, folding her arms and marching up off Main Street, her black cloak unfurled stormily behind her as though there were a great wind blowing through the relatively still morning. I watched her go with a certain amount of self-satisfaction and merriment, though I couldn't help but wonder where all this left me.

Chapter Nine

Overnight the snow had completely withdrawn from the village – as is the case with the vagaries of the weather in our part of the realm – when I arose and ventured to peer out from the lattice of my old room. It appeared that it had rained heavily during the night, but now the morning was calm and still with a sharp frost on the front lawn. I watched as several small birds fought over crumbs that a Parsonage staff member had laid out for them. Glancing at the blue-faced Church clock I noted that the time had advanced in to mid-morning, being a little after 10.30. Of course time meant little to me; we were no longer governed by the silent hands of the clock. Nevertheless, I still remonstrated with myself for slumbering on in the world of the undead! Many of you dear Readers may be asking yourself the question, "why is she not in Heaven?" but I assure you, I am! Heaven is all around you, and the myth that we deceased persons are up there high in the sky draped over golden clouds, is simply man made. I do not seek to disappoint with my revelations, but there is no such thing as the Gates of Heaven or a multitude of folk sitting before our Lord. The simple truth is we die and then we inherit the place of our death and the surrounding area. Haworth is my heaven and I have never seen my Lord. I know He is there but my time has not yet come to gaze upon the countenance of the Holy One, this can only be achieved at the Second Coming. My spirit is free to roam in the place I once called home, though not beyond the outer bounds of Haworth and its immediate moors. Believe me, dear Reader, if it were ever possible to reach Belgium and my lost love Constantin, I would not hesitate. As for my earthly husband, Arthur lies in Ireland, and I have no wish to join him. My brother Branwell I see only rarely, and my dear father, never. I do not know why this is so, or why I do not see my other two siblings, Maria and Elizabeth who passed away prematurely from their awful treatment at Cowan Bridge. My dear mother Maria and Aunt Branwell are also beyond my vision. Anne, my younger sister, lies at Scarborough and our paths never cross. Only dear Emily is my companion, in between my endless walks around the village and her roaming of the moors. Sometimes, when the mood takes me, I will accompany her on walks to the nearby moors, but mostly my interest lies in the village. I am not a moor person and never have been. My consolation lies in the appraisal of different folk I meet in my village and I never tire of seeing and hearing the various faces and languages: the Japanese people excite much interest in my soul, and I take a pride in their particular enjoyment of our stories; then come the Americans with their loud voices; closely followed by the Germans. Lesser known countries follow but I think the aforementioned nationalities are the mainstay of Haworth's international interest and economy. Emily, of course, is suspicious of those who enter our domain; she is deeply protective of our village and feels it should be invisible to outside influences. Many arguments we have had over this question, and I try to point out that without tourists our name and stories would wither away like the vine. Haworth needs the acclamation, and I need the different folk, otherwise my walks would become drear indeed! My latest dilemma, though, both excited and frightened me. I was entering a world which had mostly been denied to me, the world of real male attention, with all its vagaries. Reader, I was entering the world of romance, and I was ill-prepared for it!

At some stage of that long Christmas night that dawned into Boxing Day, I fear my mind was completely turned upside down. I awoke yearning for the strong arms of Mike, my young lawman! To him I must have appeared youthful, but I was in fact in my 39th year of age! Somehow or other, when I glanced at my reflection in a mirror or a windowpane, I had been transformed into a younger lady of around eighteen or so! I cannot offer an explanation for this, but I was indeed grateful for the gift of youth! All through my life I had been plain, yet having been honoured by a male's flattering comments about my appearance, I felt that these compliments had indeed improved my looks and uplifted my poor constitution. I glowed in Mike's infatuation of me, if that is the best way of describing the situation. As for Claire, his sister, she owned no such sentiments for me; indeed, I do believe she thought me quite mad, impersonating the 'real' Charlotte Brontë. If only the poor creature could have known the truth!

Thankfully, neither Martha nor Sally Mitchell were in evidence as I crossed over the cemetery to reach the steps of the Black Bull. Few people were about that morning, the weather being very treacherous underfoot from the previous night's sharp frost and heavy rain. The sun evinced no warmth now it was gone behind an ominous looking blanket of cloudy grey mist, and the valley itself was obliterated by dense fog. I noted that the folk who were about were well wrapped up, some complaining of intense cold as a wind rose and fell every once in a while. I felt no such chill, my spirit form oblivious to both warmth and coldness, but I still earnestly wished I could feel the painful chill of the wind if it meant I could develop my relationship with the young police officer.

I stood for a while looking up and down the quiet street; the few shops and cafes that were open were devoid of patrons and the assistants looked tired and dejected, wishing perhaps for the joys of their homes and loved ones. In my time, on Boxing Day, no such premises were allowed to open save for the druggists – much to the delight of Branwell, who's tortured mind craved such stimulants. I have no doubt that his ill health was brought on by his disastrous one-sided affair with Lydia Robinson, a parson's wife at Thorp Green, Little Ouseburn. Both my brother and sister, Anne, were employed there for some time until Branwell decided to have a tempestuous love affair with the lady of the house. I will not bore the Reader with sordid details, but I prevail upon your own judgements to acknowledge the woman was leading him on; the proof indicated by her rapid dismissal of Branwell from her life, and shortly after the death of her husband, she remarried some other person. My sisters and I have witnessed the torment of Branwell's broken love and the eventual demise of our once intelligent brother. Perhaps I may have gone the same way when M'sieur swept me from his life, had I not had my novels to fall back on and keep me company in the long hours of silence left my family's departure from life. Those were indeed awful times for me, but I came through my ordeal a much stronger person. Now, regrettably, I faced yet another love tangle!

I had no way of knowing Mike's thoughts towards me, indeed, I was not even familiar with his surname, such was the whirlwind of our meeting. I knew he was not a lawman of Haworth because the small police station had closed its doors many years ago, and so I deduced he must be a member of the Keighley Constabulary. If he never visited Haworth again then I would never know for sure, as I earlier reported to you, dear Reader, my footsteps did not allow me to wander further than Haworth or the close proximity of the moorland. If Mike wished to renew our acquaintance then he would have to come thither to me. I realised I was talking nonsense: how could her return to me if I were invisible to him!? Upon my soul, I should have to restore my normality with some haste! The one great barrier between Mike and I was Martha Clayton: without her dubious powers I had not a hope in Heaven of seeing Mike again. My realisation really hit me and my poor head began to ache. Suddenly, as if by some miracle, I noticed a brightly painted police car speeding up Main Street and towards me. I instantly recognised its driver! I stood to one side as the car pulled up by the steps and four people got out.

"And you say this figure is on the tape then?" Mike's police companion addressed a smartly dressed elderly lady. I immediately recognised her as Mrs Carrington, the manageress of the Museum gift shop; with her was Miss Leeson, her assistant.

"Yes," agreed the senior lady, "It's all there. We had an intruder yesterday whilst the Parsonage was locked up, though goodness knows how she got in or out."

"She?"

"Yes, Constable. Definitely a woman, and dressed in period costume."

"Was anything taken?" asked Mike as they proceeded to walk up the narrow alleyway.

"Not to my knowledge, no," answered Mrs Carrington.

My interest aroused, I decided to follow: I declare I saw no one in the building when I rose from slumber!

"Couldn't you have driven us around to the Parsonage car park, Constable? These pavements are very slippery you know," she complained.

Both officers said nothing.

Once in the Parsonage, the policemen were led to the main office and requested to be seated whilst Mrs Carrington dithered about with a white canvas screen.

"I thought you may as well see the film here instead of down at the station," she half-smiled, her assistant nervously holding a CCTV camera before placing it on a tripod.

"Why not simply rewind your vision screen?" suggested Mike,

"We could do... but with this device I am now setting up, the image of the intruder will be enhanced, young man!" retorted Mrs Carrington.

Unbeknown to those in the room, I stepped closer to inspect what was causing them much excitement. At first, all I saw was a room of the

Parsonage, our old entrance hall, but then suddenly a figure appeared from the direction of the stairs and walked slowly towards the front door before vanishing through the woodwork. I cried out, that figure was I! Worse still, Mike leapt to his feet and confessed he knew the person on the image!

"That young woman was sat next to me at the concert the other evening in the Sunday School! Please can you replay the tape?"

They did, with the same awesome result!

"How do you explain that then, Constable? The figure melted clean through the main entrance door!"

"This is crazy, and I know you won't believe me," cried Mike, sighing deeply, "but on the night of the performance, I offered to walk the girl home. We got as far as Bridgehouse Lane, and suddenly she just vanished into thin air!"

For a moment, the room went deathly quiet until Mike's fellow police officer asked to know the name of the figure in the film.

"She claimed she was called Charlotte."

"Charlotte?" grinned the officer, "Charlotte Brontë, you mean?" Mike's cheeks flushed a deep red.

"Search me," he said, shrugging, "she gave no surname."

"But she lived near Hall Green?" interrupted Mrs Carrington, looking over her spectacles at the beleaguered young Constable.

"The girl told me her home was on Sun Street."

"Well, that's a relief. It obviously wasn't our famous authoress then!"

"The tape must be flawed," suggested Mike's friend, "wind it back again. The girl must have had a key with her."

"I sincerely hope not, young man!" cried Mrs Carrington, "I am the only one responsible for locking up at night and setting all the alarms."

"Hey, that's a point," said Mike, scanning the short piece of film again, "Did any of the alarms need re-setting when you opened the museum this morning?"

"Not that I am aware of, no."

"Why were you in anyway? I thought the museum was closed on Boxing Day?"

"It normally is, but my assistant and I decided to do a bit of paperwork for a couple of hours."

"And you saw no one enter or leave the premises?"

"None whatsoever."

"This is all very weird," butted in the other police officer, satisfied that the film could not shed any further light on the subject. I stood by Mike, my invisible hand resting on his bright yellow coat. I stifled a laugh, even though I could not be heard! If only the people in the room could see the personage they were so worried about on the film, stood right now in their midst! It is perhaps fortunate that the elderly Mrs Carrington could not espy me, otherwise I fear the poor lady's heart would give out! With the lack of smelling salts in your modern world, it would indeed be a difficult task trying to revive her!

"Perhaps we ought to contact Marie McKuskey?" suggested Miss Leeson, breaking the silence of the room.

"Who's she when she's at home?" asked Mike's friend, rather curtly.

"Mrs McKuskey is an American psychic, she is staying locally whilst she researches for a new book she is hoping to get published."

Reader, my heart sank. If that interfering busybody actually came into contact with me – if I should be suddenly thrust back into your world – I fear she would hound me wherever I went. It was not a happy thought and I began to feel another numbing headache coming on. This may sound odd to you, my earthly Reader, but I swear we suffered just as much as if we were alive! A spirit is a spirit, but still we have human feelings. I do not know why or how this has to be, so I cannot give you a full explanation. The very mention of that American woman set me very ill at ease, even though up until this point in my tale, she had not the power or intelligence to witness my presence. I felt that this had to remain thus, that my liberty would be at stake if ever again I crossed paths with Martha Clayton: she sent me forward in time once and I doubted not she could easily do it again. I found myself teetering on the edge of a living nightmare, the sooner that American left these shores, the better! Hitherto my spiritual life had been one of freedom and joy, though now it seemed I was a marked woman on the run like some common criminal; I must escape and go find a place of safety upon the moors until the hue and cry subsided. And yet, Reader, I knew that I could not run away. Looking at the sorrow in Mike's eyes I reasoned that there had to be a way of contacting him to let him know that he was still very much in my thoughts. But how could this be achieved without the help of Martha?

Chapter Ten

A miserable day passed for me as I walked the village looking for Emily, my only thoughts being with Mike. I had left the police officers to their deliberations many hours ago and went in search of Martha's grave. Sadly, as on my previous search, I found nothing; if her grave were indeed under the sod of Haworth soil, then I did not find it. I knew that it had to be there in some quarter, because her home near Marsh fell into the jurisdiction of Haworth. The only other cemetery, apart from the new one on Penistone Hill, was a small hilltop graveyard belonging to Stanbury and I knew she could not possibly be laid there. I decided, at this point, to believe that Martha never haunted her grave but was out and about wandering the streets of Haworth, probably accompanied by her obnoxious young follower, Sally Mitchell. Having said that, I do feel obliged to inform you, the Reader, that I may be softening my stern resolve regarding that young creature now that I had myself tasted the fruits of male tenderness with Mike. To a degree we travelled the same road now, Miss Mitchell and I, and I knew and felt the keen hurt she was suffering: the love we were both so desperate for could not be reciprocated. I suspect that should I have the opportunity to extend my hand in friendship towards Mike, he would not hesitate to promote more serious feelings toward me. I do believe the poor fellow was infatuated with me!

Now the truth was out and my roving spirit had been arrested by modern technology, a fact I had hitherto been ignorant of, thinking I were totally invisible to the human eye. I worried that his material sighting of me may have changed his previously blossoming feelings towards me. I can well understand and appreciate the mental torment he was going through, after having evinced the notion that he had been wooing a timeless spirit and not a real creature of the world. Poor Mike, how he must have been teased by his colleagues back at the police station now that all were aware of his indiscretions! It is hard enough to withstand jibes and criticisms when telling of a new relationship with a normal lady, how utterly uncomfortable when all knew he was romantically involved with a dead person! I had lamentably placed poor Mike in an intolerable situation, but blame must be placed squarely in the hands of Martha Clayton, not I. I had never set out to attract a gentleman; indeed, I had not even given it credence when I began my daily walks through Haworth, I was in fact quite content to mingle, listen and follow personages I found interesting. The last thing on my mind was involvement! However, it had happened, and now I was desperate to end this futile situation. Martha's power had proven very short lived, perhaps only 3 hours at most: what kind of basis is that to let a young man pursue and court a lady?

I knew not if the power that bound me like the grip of a huge bear would return once more at the whim of the unseen woman. Maybe I would earnestly make the most of my good fortune if it did, and seek out my male suitor. Then again, perhaps not. I would look and feel a figure of mirth, walking around in my ancient clothes. No, I would have to use the advantage of darkness if I were blessed with a few more short hours of freedom with my handsome young man. And then another thought hit me, one which immediately brought on a headache: what if Martha had the power to send me forwards in time and leave me there for good? Suddenly my desire for a loving romance with Mike did not look so rosy, indeed, I felt very faint at the prospect. No matter how happy our union would be, I would have to surrender my identity and conform to your modern world; I would not be able to go about my business claiming to be the real Charlotte Brontë – that title would be lost to me forever – I would have to surrender myself to a more common surname. And if we were to marry, where would I acquire papers of identity, proof of my family life? Why would I be the only one at my own wedding ceremony? Oh my dear Redeemer, this situation is just about breaking my resolve, can I not be permitted to return to my vault in peace? Although did I truly wish to return? I think not.

I had been given a glimpse of what life really could be like, a life of love, tenderness and affection, something sadly lacking in the world I had left behind all those years ago. Mine had been a world of prudishness and self denial, a world where a parson's daughter was expected to be on her best behaviour at all times, where feelings of intimacy were to be quashed, a world of repression, religion and obedience without question. A world where one's own loving feelings were never permitted license except in the darkness of the bedroom. I have watched with horror, and a certain amount of envy, how today's young ladies conduct themselves in society:

openly flirting with strangers, kissing in public. Upon my soul! In my day, if this act were committed in open view of the public, the law breakers would be thrown into jail for indecency! Walking up Haworth Main Street on an evening, I have watched with open mouth the gropings and lewdness of male touching female, and vice-versa. In the nearby arboretum, the amount of young people indulging in acts of immorality is much worse! I have often walked away in disgust at these awful scenes of animal lust! I believe there should be a rightful place for everything, and courting should be done in a respectable manner, the girl still being a virgin on her wedding night.

***

I returned from my search of the locality empty-handed. Just when I needed my sister the most was she nowhere to be found. Unfortunately a very disagreeable person proved herself easier to find – at last! Venturing across the wide open space of the car park below my old home, came the person I had sought for many a day: Martha Clayton!

"So, Miss Charlotte, we meet at last!" she leered at me.

"You have done me much injustice, Martha Clayton. I want no more of your vile experiments, please release me at once from your wickedness!" I pleaded, but it fell on deaf ears.

"Miss Mitchell conveyed to me your liking of a certain young gentleman, Miss Brontë?"

"It is nothing. A mere infatuation on his part," I answered, feeling my cheeks begin to glow.

"Miss Sally maintains that you and he are romantically in league with each other?"

"Fiddlesticks! We have merely sat and talked!"

"About what, pray?"

"It is of no concern of yours, Martha Clayton. What we have discussed is for our ears only."

"I believe you and the young gentleman have found favour in each other's company, Miss Brontë... if I were to offer you assistance in this endeavour, would you turn your face from it?"

I was rendered speechless, and with my eyes portraying my inner feelings, I knew that the old woman would not be fooled. She knew very well that my heart yearned for human love.

"I think perhaps, Miss Brontë, I may occasion you with another chance to see your young man."

"Why are you doing this? I owe you no favours, Martha."

"Ah, but you are a famous lady and demand only the best, Miss Brontë! That rogue you married was not a patch on the young gentleman that now begs your attention; he will make a most pleasing husband for you."

"You are insane!" I cried, "how can a spirit form live with a human being? Your power over me is measured in mere hours, and then I return to the undead!"

"Ah, you are very much mistaken, Miss Brontë. Just be grateful that I am able to bring you happiness. I swear I have only given you this gift because I loved the novel you wrote – and your dear sisters – all of you are famous ladies who deserve a big reward for their endeavours at making folk happy."

"And what about Miss Mitchell and her quest?"

"Pah! She is nobbut a fool, Miss Brontë. I will never grant her wish of eternal life."

"That is most hurtful of you Martha, leading the poor girl on. She is convinced that the young man she saw outside the Black Bull is her long lost lover, Adam Sutherland."

"Well, Miss Brontë, she's late in both respects: the youth and his lady-friend have gone from Haworth before Christmas Day, and as for young Sutherland, he is to be found in a much distressed state back in his resting place."

"Distressed?"

"Aye, for not apprehending Miss Mitchell. Their paths will never cross."

"Pray, how do you know this, Martha?"

"I just do, Miss Brontë. Sally Mitchell is not worthy of my help, but you are."

"Forgive me, but I do not see why you hold this poor opinion of Miss Mitchell. Has she excited your wrath at some point in your past lives?"

"Indeed she has, Miss Brontë," scowled the old woman, "Sally Mitchell has a poor memory, but I have not! When she were nobbut fourteen, her and some school friends pelted some stones at two of my cats, injuring one of the creatures quite badly. I'll never forgive her, Miss Brontë. She comes to me pleading for help, but I always tell her untruths to make her spirit wane."

"I do not see why you cannot simply convey to her your hurt feelings, and declare no further help will be forthcoming on your part?"

"She'll learn sooner or later, Miss Brontë. In the meantime I evade her like the plague!"

Silence passed for a moment while we slowly descended Main Street. A young lady approached with a chocolate coloured Labrador, we both ignored the animal but it suddenly came to a halt before us, snarling and bearing its teeth. Despite the valiant effort of its mistress to pull it away, the animal continued to bark in our direction, its shiny coat beginning to show signs of upheaval. All we could do was watch it.

"Come on, you stupid animal, there's nothing there!" yelled the young lady, at last succeeding in dragging it away from us, but it continued to stop and look back in our direction. I fear its owner believed it quite mad! It had startled Martha to such an extent that I suddenly found myself alone on Main Street! I looked around frantically, trying to discover if Martha had made me visible again, little realising that the animal kingdom are merely excellent at picking up what is termed in your modern world as 'vibes'. I believe the dog walker would have fainted on the spot had I been unmasked, but fortunately the young woman gave no indication at having seen me. I was much relieved and gratified, but knew I had to flee from Main Street as quickly as possible for fear of becoming suddenly visible, should Martha's power over me return.

Chapter Eleven

Two weeks went by before I ventured out from my hidden lair deep within my old home. By now, the Parsonage was undergoing its closed season whilst the staff cleaned throughout and rearranged the exhibits, the precious items from our past life. I felt quite vexed one day to see one of my old, and best, dresses on display; if only I could exchange it for the plain and shabby clothes I had been condemned to wear when they interred me beneath the church floor. I was buried all in black, save for the white frill collar and sleeves had rapidly rotted away in my brief spell underground.

The Parsonage was indeed a hive of business that morning as I arose and went about my daily offices – I do not of course refer to washing and bathing, that is beyond our capabilities as spirits! We are pure from all earthly contagions and nothing may intrude on our cleanliness even in the wettest mire. Spirits do not absorb dirtiness, neither are we able to eat or drink. Well, I was at least of the fine ilk until Martha Clayton stepped into my world of the undead. In the brief hours of modern life I suffered all the vagaries of the weather and the dampness of the streets, soiling my person, my shoes, my dress; that has since passed, along with my earthly visibility.

I did so want to share precious moments with Mike, but not the pollutants that went with it, both in the streets and hostelries where cigarette smoke made me lightheaded. I much preferred my own invisible world where I was protected from all modern evils. But I could not have it on the one hand and not on the other; if I again found myself in modern day Haworth, I would have to conform. To succeed in this endeavour I started to take notice of items of ladies clothing in nearby shops, perchance I may have to suitably dress myself to avoid curious looks, but nay, they could only be had through stealing; I was not prepared to enter into a life of crime for the sake of a young gentleman friend, and he a police officer too! If our worlds collided once more, and for many a long hour, I would have to prevail upon him to supply me with agreeable clothing so as to carry off the charade of becoming a modern day Miss. However, looking at the modern clothing, I was not so sure I would agree to be dressed in such a provocative way!

All these thoughts amused me as I wandered through the busy Parsonage, watching the many hands performing different tasks to rejuvenate the Museum for its new year's opening. I noticed Emily's old, child's book of German propped up against a stout pie dish on the kitchen table, but it was never the room we once played in. It had been the Parson Wade, who had much altered our old home and built upon the gable by the lane, his extension that is now the library. I did not appreciate this intrusion on our modest home, nor did Emily, but we could do nothing about it; we had finished with our home once we passed away, let others have their way with it. The shop and courtyard, with the metal casts of us three sisters really excited Emily's wrath, complaining bitterly that it made her look ugly! Both my sisters were attractive looking ladies, I of course being the odd one out!

Coming down into the shop area, I noticed one of the staff members was about to open the door to a rather stern looking gentleman. He was dressed rather soberly in dark clothes and was carrying with him a small box from which several wires were dangling; in his other hand he appeared to be carrying a long metal pole with offshoots on, rather like the skeletal remains of a fish's body. I was quite intrigued.

"Mr Simpson, please do come in," smiled Wendy, the young girl from the office, "I see you are all prepared, I'll get Mrs Carrington at once."

"Thanks. By the way, is Mrs McKuskey here as well? I did make an appointment..."

I at once felt ill at ease, Reader, I had not bargained on the possibility of that irksome woman staying in Haworth. Seconds later she appeared, smiling, with an elegant Mrs Carrington in close attendance. They shook hands with the stony-faced gentleman and inquired whether he had had a pleasant journey. From whence he came, I know not, and never did find out, my main concern being what mischief they were planning with the odd-looking apparatus. I soon found out and the discovery sent a shiver of fear down my spine. I wanted to flee but excitement gripped me as they watched this professor plug his contraption into the shop's electricity point by means of a long spool handed over by Mrs Carrington.

"This machine is so sensitive it will pick up a spider's breathing!" boasted the man. I think not!

For safety's sake, I positioned myself behind Mrs Carrington and hoped this contraption would blow itself to pieces. I was right to be afraid. No sooner had the machine been switched on than the long finned pole the man was holding began to point at Mrs Carrington.

"Gee! Hear that cracking, Ma'am!" cried the American woman as the professor issued forth towards the stunned Mrs Carrington.

"According to this gauge I'm already picking up a reading from either in front or behind you, there's definitely a presence hovering somewhere close!"

"Oh my God!" screeched the old lady, suddenly throwing herself behind the professor.

"Got it!" he cried triumphantly, as I tried to escape the powerful probe, "It's moving towards the stairs!"

"What is? I see nothing!" exclaimed the McKuskey woman as I made haste towards the old stone staircase leading into the upper floors of the museum. To my horror I collided with a plastic gravestone that leant up against the foyer wall, the very same as used in the film 'Wuthering Heights'. It fell to the floor with a resounding smack, my pursuers suddenly rooted to the spot.

"My God!" shouted Wendy, "something has collided with Heathcliff's grave marker!"

"I told you my machine was sensitive!" cried the man, reinvigorated in his pursuit of me. I feared the worst was yet to come, Martha Clayton had picked a terrible moment to restore me to the modern world! As yet, I could not be seen, but it would only be a matter of seconds. I lifted my long dress and ran up the stairs as fast as I could, resisting the electric pull of the gentleman's machine.

I was frightened beyond comprehension as I ran into my former bedchamber and hid beneath a glass exhibit cabinet. I heard their footsteps getting ever nearer and prayed that I would not be discovered. Suddenly, a voice came to me.

"Who the hell are you, and what are you doing under there?" it was Irene Mathison, the resident cleaner of the Parsonage.

"Please, do not give me away," I pleaded, "A maniac man is chasing for me, I fear for my life!"

"Oh is he, well I'll soon deal with him!" growled the stout lady, just as the throng of pursuers reached the doorway. I had no choice but to get to my feet, there was little point in hiding now that I was once again visible.

"Who on earth is this?" demanded a flushed Mrs Carrington, "how did you get into the museum... and dressed like that?"

"I'm sorry, I came to see the librarian... our theatre is performing a Victorian play shortly – I came to... show her my outfit, if you please," I stammered.

"T'lass reckoned there were a bloke chasin' her-"

"Yes that's right, a ruffian of a fellow. He chased me all the way to the Parsonage, I fear he is now at large somewhere within the building."

"Quick, ring the police, Wendy!" shouted Mrs Carrington to her office assistant before turning back to me, "come with us to our office, we'll take care of you until help arrives."

"Thank you," I managed to mutter, as tears of shock and worry supported my supposed fear.

***

A very short while later two burly police officers arrived, with grim looks on their faces. At Mrs Carrington's instigation, a thorough search of the museum was under way, hunting for my fictional pursuer. Apart from the infuriating man with the electrical contraption, their search for a male of my description proved fruitless. The officers returned to the office, where immediate suspicion was placed at my door. One officer produced a notebook and asked for my name.

"Nicholls," I answered firmly, it would not do to mention the word Brontë! My eyes fixed upon the officer, he withdrew a little from the tenacity of my voice and my unnerving stare.

"Miss or Mrs?"

"Miss," I answered.

"Why were you hiding in the Parsonage Miss Nicholls, when we found no one who claims to see you have come in?"

"Like I told the others, I am an actress of sorts; my company hope to put on a play here soon about Victorian ladies, that is why I am dressed as such."

"And the name of your production company?"

"The Craven Valley Theatre Company," I replied at once, saying the first thing that came into my throbbing head. Mrs Carrington appeared very puzzled by my explanation and begged leave to inquire where my theatre group were based.

"A little village beyond Skipton, Ma'am."

"Personally speaking, I have never heard of your company," she eyed me warily, "but there are so many different art groups nowadays, I shall take you at your word... Now then, officer," she said, turning to my interviewer, "I am sorry we have wasted your time."

"Not at all, Mrs Carrington," he grinned briefly before looking back at me, "If the young lady would care to give us a description of the man who followed her we'll cruise around for a while to see if we can catch him."

I did indeed give an admirable description and the two officers, seemingly satisfied, excused themselves and left. I too arose and apologised before begging leave of the Parsonage staff, explaining that I was very busy and had wasted enough time.

"Don't forget to call into the library! The girls in there do all the organising for forthcoming plays in the Sunday school."

"Thank you, most sincerely," I smiled and casually made my exit, my poor heart beating like a drum as I shut the office door behind me and hurried through the shop turnstile. I had no intention of going to the library, my only thoughts concentrating on escape.

Of course, I had never given a thought to the reaction of the folk walking around Haworth, seeing this oddly dressed little woman in their midst! I was apprehended on many occasions to be asked where I got my attire from and whether they could possibly take a photograph of me. I was horrified at the prospect of appearing on some future family portrait, my invisible mask that had previously been my protector, now lain out in the dust of time. In all cases, I politely and hurriedly excused myself from their friendly company, instilling in them the urgency of my need to carry out my employment. I must declare though that I felt pangs of remorse for shunning those kind folk, but I had no choice if I wished to remain incognito.

And so it was that, instead of walking into the village, I retreated instead to Penistone Hill: out there in that broad expanse I stood a chance of hiding myself. But I had not taken into account the bitter cold of the weather, and now I was temporarily brought back into human form, I felt the keenness of the North-West wind penetrating through to my body. Where, oh where! could I seek shelter from tumult on exposed moorland? I decided I may as well walk down the hillside and along the road for a short distance, I had noticed a farm nearby with a barn full of straw. Shivering from the unexpected cold, and with my black cloak pulled firmly around me, I stumbled along the road, the wind tugging at my bonnet and trying to wrench it from my head. I knew that I would soon have to find shelter otherwise the intense cold would render me unconscious. Laughable although it may seem, I could die for a second time!

The large farm I had espied was one just over the Oxenhope road, where it dips down to Lower Laithes Dam and on to Stanbury. I heard the barking of a dog in the distance as cold and fatigue bore me on. Maybe the occupants of the farm would take pity on me and allow me succour before a hot fireplace. Whatever, I made haste across the road without looking and stepped straight into the path of a white car. The startled driver blew his horn at me as I looked up. I saw the green and yellow line of chequered squares, blue lights, and the flash of a yellow coat as the driver got out to obstruct my passage.

"Charlotte? It is you, isn't it? What the hell are you doing out here in this weather?" came a much welcome voice!

"Mike!" I smiled, almost falling into his arms.

"Come on, get into the car, you'll freeze to death otherwise!" he commanded. I laughed heartily, the young fool! Was I not beyond life already? But the interior of his conveyance was indeed warm and cosy, a far cry from my day's stage coach or landau, when all we had were blankets to ward off the worst of the Pennine weather. To hire a small gig meant no protection at all above one's head from rain, sleet, or snow; one had to endure the extreme conditions. I found the seating arrangements in Mike's car most agreeable, and the heater-thing gave off so much warmth that I felt I would soon recover. Mike drove a few yards and then parked on the grass verge.

"Right then," he smiled, "You have some explaining to do young Charlotte!"

"Do I"

"You most certainly do. Take the first night I walked you as far as Hall Green Chapel: I looked away for a moment and then you were gone! How did you do that, are you some kind of magician?"

"Perhaps it was an illusion on your part?" I smiled.

Mike leant over and gently caressed my face.

"Well you are real enough," he smiled, "so how did you escape me? Why did you escape me?"

"I fear it would trouble you too much, dear Sir, if I were to convey to you the real reason of my disappearance."

"I wish you would drop the fancy talk and get on with it, Charlotte – if that's your real name of course?"

"Of course it is!" I cried, feeling rather hurt.

"Two officers went to the Parsonage earlier today to report of someone pestering a woman dressed in Victorian clothes... I don't suppose it was you by any chance?"

"Indeed it was, but I spoke an untruth... no one but some staff members were making my life a misery."

"How?"

"They had a professor with them... he boasted that a contraption he was carrying could pick up spirits of the dead."

"And did it?"

"Yes, I rather think so."

"I don't understand where you fit into the picture... and apart from your costume that you seem reluctant to change out of since we first met before Christmas?"

"Mike, I have terrible news to impart upon you, will you please allow me your patience while I try to explain?"

"Ok," he nodded, "don't take too long though, I'm due back at the station soon."

***

During the next few minutes of delivering my epistle to poor Mike it seemed as though he were unsure of whether to laugh or cry. Every few moments his dark eyebrows arched up as more revelations were given to him. Once my story eventually concluded there came a long silence as he mulled things over in his mind. Every few moments he looked sternly at me, then out of the window, shaking his head sadly. Finally came the searing question, "You been drinking or taking drugs?" I sat there mortified as my anger rose. I made to remove myself from the car but he caught my wrist and pulled me to him.

"You are no more a ghost than my Aunt Sally!" he whispered, his lips suddenly finding mine. I felt myself tense and go into shock, Mike quickly released me and apologised. All I could do was lay back against the seat, a hand over my open mouth.

"You took advantage of me!" I squealed, my eyes fixing him with fury. But at the same time, deep inside, I felt strange, the full realisation that I had allowed a man to kiss me and my liking the brief situation!

Mike kept apologising as I lashed him with my tongue, informing him he was a brute and a heathen. But, dear Reader, I could not go on hurting him, he had stirred within me long-dead feelings of romance. I ceased my scolding in an instant, my face changing as if by a miracle, my smile ever broadening like a ripple on the surface of a river. I felt for his hand and he took it graciously, this time when he kissed me I felt my arms go about his neck. I did not resist.

"I knew you weren't a bad lass," he smiled, breaking off to kiss my forehead, "that story you told me is a work of art though, you make a fine actress, Charlotte!"

I could have railed at him again for calling me a liar, but I held my temper and begged him to believe me as I cited the incident in the Parsonage when I apparently walked straight through a door.

"So it was you? That another illusion then?"

"Indeed not, Mike. I think it was time I allowed myself to take courage and admit to you who I really am, but I warn you that I could be taken any moment from your side by Martha Clayton."

"Oh aye? Go on then Charlotte, surprise me – what the hell!"

A face had suddenly appeared at his side window, my sister Emily!

"Who the blazes are you?" cried Mike, winding down his window and noting that two ladies in period clothing were now in his company.

"I am Emily Brontë, Sir, I have come for my dear sister," smiled the dark-haired beauty who stood before him.

Mike sat there open mouthed as I removed myself from his car. I apologised, telling him that I would have to leave him for the time being. As soon as our hands touched, Emily and I vanished from sight.

Chapter Twelve

"You are not to go anywhere near Martha's old cottage or Sally Mitchell's home on Mytholmes Lane, do you hear me Charlotte?" cried Emily as she sat me down on the wall by Haworth New Cemetery and proceeded to read the riot act against me!

"What on earth possessed you to become entangled with that old washerwoman in the first place? You will occasion yourself great harm if you continue this courtship with that young lawman."

"Now shush, dear Emily, Mike deserves an explanation for all of this, the poor man must be heartbroken to see me once again slip from his arms!"

"I do not understand your feelings for this human, and we are mere spirits of our former selves; surely you must recognise that nothing substantial may be gained from your lamentable situation? You can never offer him love, nor he offer it to you – you are from different worlds!"

"I beg to disagree, Emily. Martha has given me a brief window of opportunity to share in something sadly lost in our world: the true chance of happiness!"

"Your mind is unbalanced, dear sister. For how long, pray, will you be spared to continue your growing feelings for each other? One earthly hour? Maybe two?"

"You are being a little unfair to me, Emily, I do not inform you how to conduct your own business! Why, for all one knows, you too may be enjoying a connivance with a young gentleman; you are forever out upon the heath!"

"I pray, Madam, you will withdraw that statement at once. I have no secrets to hide from you or anyone."

"Likewise, dear sister, so please let me conduct myself in the way I wish – and not by your commandment!"

***

I was furious with my sister for many a day after, and I did not see why I had to conform to her mode of decency. I had truly hit upon a raw nerve with Emily when I accused her of having a tryst with a secret gentleman; why else would she spend day after day roaming unseen on her beloved moorland? Nature cannot sustain the mind forever, there had to be another reason for Emily's joy and contentment. By the by, that was her problem, and I had a much greater one of my own: Mike!

By now it was pointless carrying on the charade of my being a real person: he had twice seen, with his own eyes, the power of the unknown. But how would I be able to face him, my young Constantin? Perhaps it would be easier if I were to simply forget him and go about my normal spiritual business? I realised in the same instant that I could not, even if I wanted to, because of the power of Martha Clayton. Any moment, at her instigation, I could be brought forward to the future again for all to see. I began to dread walking in the village, should the situation arise. I had no way of knowing for what length of time Martha's power would hold me; luckily, Emily had come along and rendered the spell useless. Then I began to wonder if she had really done me any favours by hurrying me from the arms of the young man I was becoming increasingly fond of.

Two weeks were to pass by in morose obscurity as I remained hidden unseen in my former bedchamber. I had neither the inclination nor the bravery to sally forth into the streets of Haworth, fearing the worst from the hands of Martha Clayton. Then, one day, all that changed and Mike came to me – indirectly.

I was doing my usual thing of going from room to room, watching and listening to the day visitors and taking in their comments, good and bad. As I descended the stairs, Mike suddenly walked in through the front door. I smiled radiantly at him, but of course he could not see me. For some reason he was dressed in ordinary clothes.

"Hello," said the girl on the ticket desk, recognising him, "Mrs Carrington is expecting you. Just go through that door by the kitchen, she's waiting in the office for you with that American lady."

"Oh Heavens above!" I moaned, "Is that woman still resident in the village?"

I followed closely behind Mike as he entered Mrs Carrington's private office, the McKuskey woman was already sat in place with her notebook and pen at the ready.

"Ah, P.C Gilmore! Please do come in and take a seat. Thank you for sparing the time to see us."

"No problem," smiled Mike.

"Now then young man, as I told you over the telephone, we had the CCTV film checked over for flaws and have found none. So that means we have some kind of ghost on our hands."

"And you reckon it could be the same girl I spoke to you about? But she was real!"

"Not necessarily the case," interrupted Mrs McKuskey, "it could be that your mind has temporarily blocked out your encounter with this... spectre, or whatever. The mind plays tricks on people."

"What about the video film then?"

"Ah, well, that's where the problem comes into it... Mrs Carrington and I were discussing the situation before you arrived. We both came to the conclusion that the young woman – found hiding in Charlotte's room – was the exact image of the girl in the film."

"I find that impossible to believe, Mrs Carrington," said Mike, "after all, we saw and spoke with her, she was no more a ghost than me and you are."

"Well I think there is something very strange going on in the Museum."

"What do you intend to do then?"

"I think it is time we got the newspapers and TV involved, don't you?"

"You can give it a go, Mrs Carrington, but I suspect they will think it's some kind of elaborate hoax to get more of the paying public through the Parsonage door."

"Do you believe in the spirit world P.C Gilmore?"

"I don't rightly know... I tend to keep an open mind on such matters."

"Has not this girl had some effect on you though, having been at close quarters to her and having spoken to her?"

"Not really, Mrs Carrington. To me she was just a young woman with a fetish for dressing in Victorian costume."

"Well, I have checked the name of her supposed theatre company and it does not exist!"

"Then why hang around the Parsonage?"

"I do not know the answer to that question, P.C Gilmore. But if and when the press get involved, I would be most grateful if you backed me up on my ghost theory."

"How can I do that," smiled Mike, "when I was not here the other week when she was apprehended? One of my colleagues happened to pat her on the shoulder when she was tearfully trying to describe the man said to be chasing her, if she hadn't been real I'm sure he would be tripping over himself to tell everybody at the station!"

"Hmm, I suppose so," mused Mrs Carrington, biting her lip. "This is very infuriating! We have two girls dressed in identical Victorian costume, and one of whom is capable of melting through a solid door!"

"Have you noticed anything out of place before now?"

"In what way, Constable?"

"Figures – or a figure – haunting the place?"

"None whatsoever! I'm sure if that were the case my staff would flee the Parsonage!"

"Don't forget the library incident, Ma'am?" interrupted Mrs McKuskey.

"What? Oh, yes, I'd forgotten... one of the girls working there complained that when she sat down her seat felt like a block of ice and yet there was a high humidity count in the room."

"So what are you suggesting, Mrs Carrington? A haunted chair?"

"You may laugh P.C Gilmore, but the librarians were so scared that they fled from the room."

"Me too, Buster!" laughed the American lady.

"So when you eventually decide to approach the press with this story, I imagine you will want to link both the incidents, in that the ghostly woman was haunting the library?"

"Indeed, Constable!"

"Are you suggesting the phantom could be one of the Brontë sisters?"

"Hardly likely: the building that houses our library was not built when the Brontë's were alive."

"Oh right, so if it were a ghost then it could be a relative of the next parson, Rev. Wade?"

"You are very knowledgeable about the Parsonage, I congratulate you, Constable!" laughed Mrs Carrington.

"Like everyone else around Keighley, I was forced to learn about the Brontë family at school."

"Although you don't sound particularly enthusiastic, you could do worse things, Constable."

"Yes," chuckled Mike, "like dating a Haworth girl!"

"Really? Who is the lucky lady, do we know her?"

"I doubt it, she doesn't hang about the village too much, her job takes her all over the place."

"Oh? What is her occupation?"

"Freelance journalist."

I chuckled to myself when I heard that white lie escape my young friend's lips, journalist indeed! Looking at Mike, I sensed that he knew I was not far away listening in to this conversation, his eyes constantly flickering round the room for some sign. I would have given anything in that moment to be able to stand beside him and say 'yes, we are good friends'. Unfortunately Martha's power was not in evidence, but I believe it to be very providential because had I suddenly materialised from thin air and admitted to a stunned assembly who I was, I can only guess what the headline would be in the local newspaper! It was best to remain vigilant and careful.

Chapter Thirteen

After a further hour of deliberation the little party broke up and went their separate ways. I decided to follow Mike. By now, my heart was breaking, having no ability to suddenly reappear to the young man I knew that I was hopelessly falling in love with! At first I tried to tell myself that it was all nonsense, and nothing could come of our union; yet as my feelings grew for Mike, I rebelled against Reason and demanded to be reinstated in his arms. Unfortunately, Martha's power was full of defects and there was no certainty as to when, if ever, I would be able to begin my relationship with the young lawman.

As we walked down the lane to the church, I observed the hurt in Mike's eyes, the hunched shoulders and the tautness of his lips, full of despair and longing for a young lady who had the ability to skip in and out of his life at will. I felt so sorry for him, but I was powerless to intervene. Then, suddenly, to my astonishment, Mike began talking to himself... but to me!

"I know you are there Charlotte, even though I can't see you," he said, looking up briefly. "For what it's worth, you might like to know I have real feelings for you. I don't see you as a ghost or whatever, even though this situation is pure crazy! I just want you and need you."

My lips trembled, dear Reader, and I felt the moisture begin to form around my eyes; I felt the privation of belonging to someone but not being able to touch or embrace them. We were as two lovers separated like convicts behind an impenetrable iron railing. I felt both devastated and angry that it had come to this, my finding someone to truly love me and yet not being able to act upon that love. All my life, in the 1800s, I had sought and yearned for such love only to be disappointed. True, my earthly husband, Arthur Bell-Nicholls, had loved me in his own way, but this was nothing that I felt in comparison to the warmness and security I felt with Mike. There had to be a way around this situation, and somehow I am certain that this had all been pre-planned for us – not by Martha, a mere go-between – but by a much higher authority in Heaven. Martha was just like me, a mere spirit amidst a multitude of other roaming lost souls that inhabited the earth, and for the most part, unseen by the human eye. Now it seemed that I had been the chosen one to take part in some unknown experiment to determine what happens when earthlings and spirits cross paths! I was thus engrossed with my problem when suddenly I realised Mike had gone from my vision! I desperately looked around, finally spotting him going through the turnstile at the western end of the cemetery that leads to the moors. I quickly ran after him, lifting my trailing skirts. I shouted his name like a fool, calling to him several times, and yet I knew he could not hear me. I ran on like someone demented, my quarry quite oblivious to my plight. At best I could walk beside him, and at worst I could turn my back forever on him and return to my haunting ways and dull spirit life. I could not do that, both of us had come too far forward in our unreal relationship; we needed each other.

I eventually drew breathlessly alongside my young beau, he not aware of my discomfort. He walked now at a brisk pace as we ascended up the stone track that lead to the old quarries on Dimples Lane. Several other folk passed us by and he briefly acknowledged them, he now seemed in much better spirits. Perhaps the recent interrogation had weighed deeply on his mind; if he had parted with too much information he could have been scorned or – at worse – deemed unfit for his profession for imagining he had talked with a 'ghost'. Mike's position was indeed precarious, and I had been responsible for this. I felt really exhausted by it all, and forlornly hoped for a solution. I only had two choices: one, to run away; or two, carry on with this impossible courtship. The second option it had to be though, I was a woman with romantic needs and I craved both physical and mental love, although the former was perhaps impossible!

Since first meeting Mike I often wondered what it would feel like to make love with another man. In Arthur's case, he had been the Taker in our marriage and I did my duty out of necessity, I shared few romantic feelings with him as he physically entered me. Even though I was the author of the deeply passionate novel Jane Eyre, in real life passion was not what I had expected it to be. I found physical love with my husband durable, but lacking in every sense, I was not fulfilled. With Mike, even though we had never reached that final stage of our relationship, he simply set my heart racing like no other and whenever he came near me, held me, kissed me, I found myself responding to his demands. I felt the sensation known as ecstasy and I longed for the moment of complete intimacy. But I may have to suppress my feelings forever, unless something miraculous happens. Reader, I had no sooner allowed this thought to escape from my head than I felt a jolt go right through my entire body! Mike leapt back and almost tripped over himself, had not a dry stone wall come to his rescue!

"Charlotte!" he yelled, then lurched towards me; in a thrice we were in each other's arms our lips hungrily pressing into each other, my arms around his neck. Finally we broke away and I stepped back from him a little, my hands outstretched in his strong grip.

"I didn't dare to hope you would come back to me, now that we both know the truth about you," he spoke tenderly, his eyes boring into mine. I felt my legs go weak, his smile I could never resist, I never wanted to resist... I was in love, totally and unashamedly. Only time and the world separated our mutual feelings. Mike was no fool, he understood our dilemma: in an instant I could be gone from him, maybe never to return. But for this magical moment, we had each other. Every moment must be cherished, every kiss, every emotion I could muster from my long lifeless body.

"Charlotte, you are so real... so wholesome," he said, reading my thoughts. "How is it possible that I can hold you, feel the warmth of your skin, see your lovely smile?"

"Please, Sir, you allow me too many compliments. I am but a plain young woman, ageing before her time-"

"Now, stop it!" he ordered, pulling me to him, "beauty is in the eye of the beholder. Charlotte, you have a beautiful face, silky rich hair, you are perfect!"

I burst out laughing and playfully pushed him away.

"I fear your eyes are of a delicate nature, Sir. They are incapable of seeing the truth about me, I fear..." I trailed off, his embrace tightening around me, his lips and body pressed into mine; I felt like swooning! Never before have I felt such excitement flash through my body like this; it was enough for me to stop myself taking things one step further, my body aching so much for this young man who could free my tormented soul. Mike must have shared the very same thoughts, I felt his hands begin to touch the upper half of my body. Suddenly, the spell was broken and I pushed him away, telling him gently that out here in an open lane was not the place I would choose for intimacy. My stern rebuke brought him back to his senses and he humbly apologised and then suggested we find somewhere more private.

***

A long time later, we sat in the warmth of some bales of straw we had come upon in a farmer's barn close to 'Sowdens', a farm once lived in by the colourful vicar of Haworth, Rev. Grimshaw. No one, save for some inquisitive sheep feeding nearby, had witnessed our stealthy approach and disappearance into the dark confines of the old building. A rickety ladder had given us private access to an upper chamber and it was there that I experienced my first act of physical love with Mike. It was neither rushed nor animalistic; Mike was indeed a gentle and caring man, and I sighed with contentment when it was over and we lay in each other's arms, quietly looking up at the ceiling beams. Eventually Mike broke the silence, declaring that he thought this experience was all a dream that he would soon awake from, upset and broken hearted.

"No, dearest," I soothed, reaching above my head to ruffle his little black beard. "We are together for now, you and I, let us not discuss the future."

"Like take one day at a time, you mean?"

"Absolutely, maybe even one hour, for I know not whence I shall be taken back to my own world."

"I still cannot offer a rational explanation as to how you are able to take on your earthly body after all these years and then, just as quickly, leave it."

"That is the work of Martha Clayton, I fear... I have no defence against it."

"Do you realise, Charlotte, that woman must be as powerful as God himself. To be able to dictate who and who will not live again."

"I believe Martha's power does indeed flow from our Creator: I also believe our union has been pre-planned for years. Why should I be allowed this happiness I am now enjoying with you? I have done nothing to deserve it apart from carrying out my basic Christian duty. Do you believe in the afterlife, Mike?"

"Not up until now, no!" he smiled, kissing the top of my head. "I tend to keep an open mind... I mean, no one has ever come back from the dead to claim there is a Heaven out there?"

"I beg pardon to remind you that I have, my love!"

"Yes, Charlotte, I don't need reminding!" he grinned, tickling my sides. Suddenly I was on my feet, laughing hysterically. I hated being tickled! However, I did make an exception for Mike. He too, got up and began chasing me around the hayloft, me screaming and tripping over my long dresses to get away from him. Our exuberance knew no bounds as he pretended to nearly catch me, only to let me go again. This time though, I hurriedly scrambled down the ladder with Mike in hot pursuit, all the time both of us laughing gaily.

"Hoi!" a sudden stentorian voice broke the spell, "What d'you two think you're playing at? This is private property!"

As one, we froze on the spot.

"Just larking about," smiled Mike, trying to apologise.

"I ought to get t'Bobbies on you two..." glared the weather-beaten red faced man, wearing a farmer's overcoat.

"Waste of time, pal!" grinned Mike, producing his police identity wallet. The old farmer's jaw dropped open as Mike sought and took my hand. "No harm done, we're just leaving."

"Well dang me!" cursed the man, watching our hasty retreat. "I've a good mind to report you olt son!"

"Suit yourself!" retorted Mike as we ran laughing across the open pasture, scattering the poor sheep.

Chapter Fourteen

As we happily made our way over the moor to the old quarries on Penistone Hill, Mike and I had no idea the furore we would unleash by our romantic tryst in the barn. The farmer wasted no time in letting all the locals know about the young police officer gambolling in the hay with an oddly dressed woman! News would eventually reach the ears of old Mrs Carrington who alerted the police in Keighley, fearing that Mike was involved in some sort of elaborate plan to rob the Parsonage of all its precious treasures! But that was in the week hence, and for now, Mike and I bathed in our newfound love.

The quarries on Penistone Hill, just to the West of Haworth, have long been silent and unused as nature's vegetation slowly claims back its countryside. One can still walk along the old valleys hewn from the rock face by a gang of long-dead quarry men. In total there were three quarries here, the largest being Jagger's which is where we now found ourselves. Apart from us there was not a soul about save for the odd curlew that soared aloft on the air currents, its sharp melodious cry reaching our ears. The winter's day was beautiful, sunny with clear skies and not a breath of wind to ruffle the peace of the desolate quarry.

"Did you ever come into contact with any of the men who once worked in here?" asked Mike as we steadily walked along, hand in hand.

"My sister Emily was always here, talking to the quarrymen at every opportunity!" I laughed.

"D' you reckon that's where she got her ideas from... her Heathcliff maybe?"

"What, are you intimating that Emily was having a secret liaison with one of the men?"

"Yeah but you did once make a reference to Emily's boyfriend, saying he might be connected to the quarries?"

"I think I also suggested he was a gipsy, did I not?"

"Whatever, I reckon your sister had plenty of opportunities to court a man from here."

"Emily took the secret to her grave, and even now in our world of spirits, she will not convey to me what really happened up here on these moors."

"It has been suggested that your sister may have been pregnant when she died?"

"Fiddlesticks, Mike! Upon my soul, I have never heard such nonsense! Where did you hear such poppycock?"

"I read a magazine article once... someone else even went as far as to say she was a lesbian?"

"Oh for pity's sake, Mike! Now you really have excited my anger – not at you – but the person who printed such a spurious epistle! My poor sister was not involved in either situation you have mentioned, believe me!"

"Your word is good enough for me, Charlotte. Anyway what are we to do about our own problem, more to the point?"

"I fear that nothing can be done, Sir. We just go on hoping for the best but fearing the worst."

"If I knew for certain that you could remain here for good I'd set you up home with you someplace, get you proper clothes and a new identity."

"That would be most agreeable dearest, but I fear it is all a dream on both our parts; much as I would love to spend my time with you, we both know that my sudden exit from your world can come at any moment."

"Do you get some sort of warning Charlotte?"

"Indeed! It is like a bolt of lightning searing through my body. I feel no pain, but the experience renders me quite weak."

"That would be Martha's power coming through, I expect?"

"Indeed so, Mike... Oh, how I wish she would send me to you and then leave me in peace for eternity!"

"Why does she single you out, Charlotte? Have you upset her in the past?"

"Not to my knowledge. I fear the woman looks upon me as her heroine, having studied Jane Eyre and declared me a saint for women!"

"I wonder how many other people she has cast a spell on."

"I know of at least one," I replied, linking arms with Mike as we ascended a steep slope out of the quarry workings.

"Oh yes, do I know her?"

"I fear not, Sally Mitchell was a product of Victorian Haworth."

"What's her story then?"

"Sally was in love with one Adam Sutherland. Theirs was a doomed relationship from the beginning: she was with child almost straight away, forcing her parents to part the two lovers."

"I thought that in your time, men who got girls pregnant were then obliged to marry them?"

"That is generally true, but in this case it is believed Sally's family had Adam murdered and his body buried in a shallow grave upon the moor."

"Heck! Was this ever proven?"

"No, Sir. At least not whilst I was alive"

"So, this Sally, is she being helped by the Clayton woman?"

"Only half-heartedly," I said, going on to explain the cat incident.

"And this Adam chap? Have you ever come across him in your world?"

"Oh, indeed! I have acquainted myself with him on several occasions, and I find him to be quite a likeable gentleman."

"Look, Charlotte, I know this question will sound corny to you, but do spirits ever get into a romantic relationship with each other?"

"Unfortunately, not!" I laughed.

"So... with me, it's a whole new experience for you then?"

"Agreeably so, Sir!"

"How will your Emily take it?"

"I fear she will have to get used to the situation."

"I still can't believe I'm talking like this – asking a ghost about their life story! Maybe I'm not, maybe I'm simply talking to myself?"

"Does my hand upon yours not seem real then, my love?" I asked tenderly.

We stopped talking and looked at one another a few moments and then kissed. Once again I allowed myself to be lowered to the ground, Mike exploring my body beneath my dress. A moment more and we were once again joined at the hip by the act of physical love. This time it was more demanding and I felt pain as Mike took me, but it was the pain of love, not hurt, and I could well endure it.

When our union was over, Mike rolled off me, his breath coming in short rasps and his eyes closed tightly. I got up and brushed grass off my long dress and then, bending over him, I smiled and began to lower myself onto his stomach. In that instant the wretched Martha Clayton once more ordered me back to my world! I felt anger, hurt, and humiliation all rolled into one. I cursed her for the evil creature she was. Poor Mike!

That night, and for many after, my sleep was tortured by recurring bouts of depression at losing my man. These brief interludes of bliss could not go on: either Martha Clayton revised her powers and sent me forwards to the future forever, or she released me to carry on where my previous life had left off, a silent witness roaming the modern world. The present situation was intolerable, I hated the thought of continuing crossing from one dimension to another, at the whim or insistence of an old woman.

Chapter Fifteen

I recommenced my solitary walks around my home and village, mainly on the alert for my young policeman. I laughed heartily to myself at the recollection of Mike's words of concern when we finally ceased lovemaking and prior to Martha reclaiming me. He had suggested we had played with fire, he not taking any precautions about impregnation! I laughingly told him that the mother of all miracles would have to be used to allow me to get into that situation, even though my body had taken earthly form during our brief courtship!

Mike was a very caring young gentleman, if a little insecure. Maybe he was reflecting on his real-life trysts with other young ladies, and the fear of unwanted pregnancy? Whatever, it was never going to happen with me! That was the beauty of our strange, physical relationship: we could do anything and get away with it. Avoiding people would prove much more difficult, I fear.

***

On my unseen journey back up Main Street my excitement was aroused somewhat by the discovery that Mike's sister, Claire, was walking in front of me with one of the Parsonage staff. It was around time for luncheon and I noticed the two young ladies emerging from Haworth Tea Rooms. I quickly caught up with them and walked alongside Andrea, who was one of the museum guides. Claire was walking slowly, with arms folded and a tense expression on her face. It would seem I had stumbled upon them at a most opportune moment!

"Will your brother have to face an enquiry?" asked Claire's companion.

"I don't think so, but Mike's Superintendent made it quite plain that he was being carefully watched."

"As if Mike would steal anything from the Parsonage!"

"You know what the police are like, once they suspect you of the littlest thing... even when it's one of their own officers!

"Will Mike be taken off the squad car team?"

"No Andrea, they haven't got enough evidence to accuse him of anything."

"What about that old farmer, d'you think he was making up the story for attention?"

"No, Mike admitted he had been with a girl dressed in costume."

"Bit embarrassing for him! I wonder who she is?"

"If you ask me Andrea, I reckon the girl is off her trolley... going about dressed as a Victorian."

"I suppose she would not have looked too out of place around Christmastime, though."

"No, I don't suppose she would... but it's mid-January now!"

"D'you know her, Claire? Does she live local?"

"She told Mike she lives on Sun Street but then wouldn't let him take her all the way home, said something about her Dad getting uptight about her seeing a copper."

"But he wouldn't have known, Mike was in civvies the night of the performance at the Sunday school, wasn't he?"

"Yeah, but Mike's work would have been bound to come up in conversation sooner or later if he had been invited to her house."

"Well why's her Dad against the police?"

"I don't know... maybe he's had a few run-ins with the law?"

Silence for a moment.

"Will Mike see her again, now all this has come out?"

"Oh definitely, he's mad on the lass."

"And you don't like her?"

"She's shifty, Andrea... not to be trusted."

"Why d'you say that?"

"Well, any girl walking around every day in Victorian costume is a bit odd. I reckon the girl is mentally unbalanced."

"Has Mike said anything about her clothes?"

"Yes, several times apparently. But all she says is that she feels comfortable in them."

"Sounds to me like one of those New Age people?" grunted Andrea.

I let the two ladies go, I had heard quite enough to render me weak in the head; no wonder I had not seen Mike since, the poor creature must be laying low and keeping out of mischief. But I needed him to be here with me, even though he could not see me. I could maybe give him some sort of sign – like when my dress threw the papers on the carpet in the library. If

Mike knew that I was within easy reach of him, all would be well. He could talk to me even though in my present form I could not answer back. That did not matter so much as he not being in Haworth at all. It was no good wishing, dear Reader, Mike would not come when I commanded or desired; I would have to be patient. Worse was to follow.

One week hence of Mike's interrogation by his aloof superiors, who had not the ability to see the truth even if it were thrust in their faces, we had quite a distinguished man of the cloth visit our Parsonage. I only became aware of him as I descended the old hallway stairs one afternoon, shortly after the museum had closed its doors on the day visitors. He was stood in deep discussion with Mrs Carrington who seemed want to keep pointing this way and that, and finally at the front entrance door.

"According to the CCTV camera, the phantom appeared from the direction of the servant's room, am I correct?"

"That is so," nodded Mrs Carrington.

"Could it not then be the soul of one of those servants, as opposed to a Brontë sister?"

"Yes, I suppose it could, Rev. Whitham."

"And what did your young policeman friend say about it? I understand he spoke to a young lady dressed exactly as the figure on the film?"

"P.C Gilmore was most insistent that the young lady was a genuine person, a little odd in dress sense, maybe, but a very real person."

"Did she supply him with a name?"

"Yes, it was Nicholls, Charlotte Nicholls."

"Good Lord!" cried the reverend, his dark eyebrows raised. "You do realise that was the name given to Charlotte Brontë on the occasion of her marriage to her father's curate?"

"Now come along Rev, you're surely not suggesting that the blurred image on the film is that of Charlotte Brontë?"

"It is possible, Mrs Carrington."

"I hardly think so... the girl P.C Gilmore escorted home that night lived down the hill on Sun Street."

"So P.C Gilmore took her right to her front door?"

"No, not quite. The girl made some excuse about having an angry father who was insanely protective of men chatting up his daughter, especially police officers!"

"Aha! That could have been a ploy to ward off suspicion of her."

"Well, why? For what reason?"

"If she really were Charlotte, she wouldn't want to give her secret away to anyone."

"Oh, stop this nonsense at once!" cried Mrs Carrington, her lined face quite red. "P.C Gilmore spoke to the girl and held her hand, hardly a ghost wouldn't you say?"

"Trick of the mind dear lady, P.C Gilmore could have been under some hypnotic trance, imagining that he saw and touched the girl."

"Then what about the other folk who have come forward to testify that they too saw her sat by the Constable in the Sunday school? Not to mention the latest offering from the farmer, how do you explain that?"

"At present, I cannot... but there is a logical explanation for everything, Mrs Carrington. However, our first priority is to allow me to exorcise this whole building."

"Exorcise!" I screamed, my anger rising within me like the flaming contents of a volcano about to erupt.

"No!" I shouted, darting around the hallway like someone from a lunatic asylum. My inner power must have triggered off something else more destructive: pictures began to fly off walls and the girl sat by the ticket office was sent reeling to the floor with her chair on top of her. Mrs Carrington screamed and hid her face from the tumult.

Her scream made me come to my senses; I withdrew to a corner of the passageway and surveyed the scene of total destruction. There were fragments of broken glass everywhere and some had found a home in the head of the bald parson. A member of staff, hearing the commotion, had appeared and helped tend the vicar's wounds, which were bleeding quite seriously. The girl lying on the floor at the ticket kiosk groggily gained her feet and helped the dazed Mrs Carrington. All around her lay the dust and debris, it looked as though a whirlwind had gone through the place.

"Poltergeist!" shouted Rev. Whitham, "we have to get help at once!"

"Oh my Lord!" I cried, my hand covering my lips as I looked around at the damage I had caused. Even the old Grandfather clock that my father had wound up every night on his way to the bedchamber now lay on its side, its glass face smashed into segments across the landing.

“This is not me, I have no power!” I kept screaming to myself. In that awful moment, before I fled from my former home, I realised what evil Martha Clayton had bestowed upon me, having tried to convince me that she was helping me find happiness!

The thought that I was now in league with the Devil filled my every movement as I rushed out of the Parsonage and stood at a distance as a crowd began to gather. I could not believe I had caused so much hurt to people in so short a burst of anger. Martha Clayton held me in a vice-like grip and I had been unaware of her sinister powers of wanton destruction while my temper had been agreeably calm. Now I saw at firsthand what I had allowed myself to get into. I should have known – as I suspected at the start – that if I went in search of easy happiness there would be a price to pay. My dear family would have been appalled by my outburst of destructive energy, had they witnessed it. To all, I was generally a mild-mannered person and slow to anger. I fought back tears at the realisation of what a monster I had become. Martha Clayton would have to be stopped before further outrages were committed by myself, with no defence against her.

By the time the police and ambulance people had arrive on the scene, a large crowd had converged on the Parsonage and filled the front lawn. I did not see Mike in their number, but I was too distraught with myself to care at that moment in time. I did hear, however, a comment from two persons walking back down the cemetery path, that a noise like thunder had emitted from the museum and had falsely alerted people to believe there had been a gas explosion. I felt weak and disorientated, I even contemplated giving myself to the police for the crime I had committed. But no one would have seen me if I had walked forward, I was invisible to all. Thankfully, Martha Clayton’s hold over me was not evident in that moment. I deemed it necessary to put myself at as much distance from the Parsonage as I could for the time being.

***

Hours later found me quite miserable and forlorn on a seat inside the Villette cafe. I had decided to seek shelter from prying eyes in the street and hide away in one corner of the building. When I said prying eyes, I of course referred to Martha Clayton, but to my distress it was Sally Mitchell who found me, and she had a young gentleman with her.

"Miss Brontë?" she smiled, "I am quite surprised to find you seeking shelter in this busy parlour, have you not heard about the calamity up at the Parsonage?"

"I do not understand, why is Mister Sutherland with you?" I choked, ignoring her question.

"Why, my dear old Martha restored him to my side many days ago; we are indeed very happy together."

"Martha convinced me that she was not going to help you because of what you did to one of her cats all those years ago?"

"I fear Martha is playing games with you, Miss Brontë!" laughed Sally as she sat down beside me to gloat. Adam remained standing.

"I was responsible for the situation at the Parsonage," I said glumly.

"You?"

"Yes, I lost my temper when I heard a reverend announce he was going to exorcise the place. I cannot allow that to happen, Miss Mitchell, it is sacrilege to our home."

"But no one haunts the place except you?"

"Emily comes back from time to time."

"I do not understand you: how could you be responsible for all the damage inflicted?"

"Have you seen it for yourself?"

"Yes, Miss Brontë, I have."

"Well, as I say, it was I who caused it; I lost control of my senses and something evil in me took over."

"Not you, Miss Brontë... I suspect another being was responsible, totally separate from you. Someone who needed an excuse to destroy your former home, someone like Martha herself."

"Martha?" I cried, "why would that woman seek revenge upon our family?"

"Why indeed? She told me she hated all your family in real life, she was insanely jealous of your literary success."

Suddenly I felt nausea flood me. To think that I had been fooled into believing Martha Clayton had only my best interests at heart, when all this time she had been plotting my downfall!

"Do not concern yourself too much, Miss Brontë, I am obliged to inform you that she intimated to me that she is quickly tiring of her game with you, and is contemplating moving her interests to destroy some other poor soul who excites her distaste."

"Martha Clayton is a wicked and evil woman; she must be stopped in occasioning any more harm to the innocents. I shall have to tax myself over this issue and call on the help of a higher authority."

"But where will that leave you, Miss Brontë... concerning your... gentleman friend?"

My heart sank: where indeed? Without Martha's powers of transportation I would be doomed to never walk, talk or hold Mike again! Sally's timely warning served only to bring forward another excruciating headache, similar to what I had experienced in real life. I was now the victim of circumstance, and whichever way I turned, Martha was at the centre of my nightmare. True, I was now free to roam wherever I wished without the fear of being exposed, but I had sampled the fruits of your modern world and I wanted more!

Chapter Sixteen

Amidst much publicity, and the presence of the press and a TV company, the Parsonage was duly exorcised once Rev. Whitham had recovered from his injuries. I stood at a respectful distance in the crowded lane but overheard every word spoken inside of my old home. Several learned gentleman who boasted they were ghost hunters accompanied Rev. Whitham inside along with other local dignitaries, church leaders and interested member of the press, TV and radio. Of course, the fools found no one to vent their claimed powers of good upon: I had already warned Emily to stay well away from our home until the hue and cry had died down. She had thanked me for my timely advice, whilst lambasting me for being such a fool as to allow my temper license in the presence of mortals. To her, I was a complete and utter product of wanton lust. She did not realise that, like her, I had feelings for a man. Emily prided herself on her ability to keep well clear of any modern world situations. She would quietly conduct herself – and, I believe, her love-life – away from prying eyes, in the quiet desolation of the moors. I could not take such cover; if I wanted to court my gentleman I would have to face the streets of Haworth and run the risk of being exposed. Now though, even that had been taken from me.

***

Winter soon retreated into Spring, if that be the right term to describe Haworth at the opening of a season of growth and new life in the countryside, with the harsh winds coming in from a North-Westerly direction doing nothing to make the sufferer believe that Spring had indeed arrived, despite the profusion of daffodils and early crocus. The icy blast still battered the stout walls of my former home and invaded the alleyways near the church. As for myself, I could not feel the power of the relentless wind, my senses no longer numbed by its chillness. I knew of its existence because it ruffled my hair and plucked at my petticoats and made my thick cloak billow out behind me as I stood at the top of Penistone Hill, looking out over the domain of my fiery sister. Today the moors were at their bleakest, the sun an occasional visitor to this wasteland of broken dreams and heartache, only the robust sheep with their thick woolly coats seemed to derive much pleasure from our rude hills.

Presently, I relaxed my vigil and began the short walk back to Haworth. There was not a soul to be seen on the moorland path even though there was much evidence of humans, judging by the rows of parked cars on the edge of the valley. As I gained the road, a person – a young lady – issued from one of these contraptions. She had in her possession a large camera which hung around her bare neck, and her warm coat was open to the waist revealing a white cardigan and jeans. On her feet were dark hiking boots. As I watched she heaved onto her back a large bag of some description, and then proceeded to set off in the direction of Haworth a clipboard and pen in her hands.

How strange, I thought; should she not be pointing in the direction of the moors rather than the built up village? Little did I realise that this young woman was about to step into my life, that all my waking moments would be focused on her, and she would eventually free me from repression at the hands of Martha Clayton. But more of that much later. The first time I came into contact with Miss Joanna Thurnscoe I little realised what an impact she would have on myself, and on my lover, Mike, a gentleman sadly lacking from my life of late. From the time of the exorcism Mike had never graced Haworth with his presence, my heart felt broken as I sadly concluded our strange affair had come to a dismal end. If he said he loved me, as he had so often professed, why did he not avail himself to me more often? I suspect his career took precedence overall and he wished to distance himself from the strange 'little woman' of Haworth. Even then, I was not fully convinced he really did believe me to be Charlotte Brontë.

Back, then, to the young lady in question. Joanna had lovely, long, ginger hair, naturally curly I suspect, that fell off her head and halfway down her back in luxuriant texture. Her forehead was parted like my own, but her small face was much more attractive and she owned the most exquisite ice blue eyes and interesting nose. Her lips were rather spoiled though by too much make up, as was the case with the dark blue mascara on her eyelashes. Her height, I would suggest, was little more than five feet and she was very slim with a neat little bust.

We walked along side by side, she totally unaware that a famous person was only inches from her side as she hummed a tune. I noticed her name from the outset because it was clearly marked on a lapel badge she had pinned to her cardigan, but it gave no further details as to what organisation she belonged to. I liked what I saw though, and deemed her a most pleasant and respectable young lady. Our journey was brought to a temporary halt by the walled path that fringed Haworth rectory on West Lane. Joanna stopped abruptly and jotted down some notes before taking a photograph. Satisfied, she once again headed in the direction of Haworth, and the Parsonage.

It was quite obvious that she had not been to Haworth before, judging by the many occasions she briefly stopped to take more photographs, but as we arrived outside of the Parsonage gift shop my friend's face really lit up. She snapped away like there was no tomorrow and then walked forwards towards the main gate to the museum. However, here her exuberance waned somewhat when she took notice of the admission fee to go in! Like many before her, Joanna deemed it impractical and time-consuming spending her hard earned money to walk around a modest museum. Instead, she sighed heavily and then made her way down the lane toward the cemetery. She took yet more pictures as she noted a signpost that was subject to Japanese tourists only. I too had to smile, I could hardly begin to wonder what Papa or Branwell would have made of it all, these oriental visitors swarming through our village and moorland! Presently, Joanna tired of taking her pictures and placed the camera inside her bag. Looking around, she suddenly placed herself on the flat surface of a gravestone and proceeded to peel a banana!

"Upon my soul!" I cried, "What bad manners indeed, feasting above the remains of a long dead person!"

Suddenly I noticed part of the inscription to the sleeping occupant beneath: 'In Loving Memory of Martha Ann Clayton, who died in the thirty seventh year of her age...' My heart skipped a beat as I repeated the wording; all this time I had searched diligently for the grave and yet I must have walked past it numerous times without realising! Well now at least I would come face to face with my tormentor at last, once she returned from her wanderings. Thank you Miss Joanna!

About five minutes later my young friend got to her feet and walked off. I peered briefly down at the moss covered grave marker and then followed her. I was intrigued by her passion to take so many pictures; I felt there was more I needed to know about her. And then quite an unexpected thing happened. Coming down the stone steps in front of the church Joanna dropped her clipboard, her blue writing pen rolling away over the stone setts. In an instant I found myself retrieving it for her, not realising I had either the power or ability to do so, it being a normal reaction. I almost fainted from shock when I realised Joanna – and others – could actually see me! There had been no warning, no sudden charge of power through me. It came as a tremendous blow, and I feared the worst possible reaction, but Joanna smiled radiantly and thanked me as I shakily handed back her pen.

"Who are you, girl?" she exclaimed, complimenting me on my 'unique' costume, as she put it.

"I am... err... just a normal being," I smiled nervously.

"Great outfit! Are you acting in a play or something?"

"No, I simply dress thus to impress the visitors," I lied.

Well, what else could I do? I was hardly likely to confess my true identity to a total stranger. Even if I had I fear I would be laughed off the street by all; my appearance had drawn quite a crowd of inquisitive folk around us, some taking photographs of this strange girl in their midst who was dressed up in Victoriana.

"You seem quite a celebrity?" smiled Joanna, taking out her own camera.

"I think it best if we escaped to a more discreet location, I am not one to be used as an object of interest," I scowled, looking around me at all the different faces.

"Ok," said Joanna, taking my arm and leading me back up the church steps.

"Where are you taking me?"

"I thought perhaps back to my car for a little chat... if you have no objection of course?"

"No, of course not my dear, that would be most agreeable."

***

A short while later, with a watery sun streaming in through the car's windows, Joanna told me all about her life as a freelance journalist for a ladies magazine. Her work contained romantic storytelling that was based on real folk. I felt very at ease and relaxed in her pleasant company, after all, here was a lady writer after my own ilk, if not on a much lower scale than I had been. All the same I felt honoured to be allowed into her private world, but when it came to my turn I fear I told a few little untruths in regard to my daily occupation and mode of work! Joanna settled on the notion that I was a person dressing up to raise money for some worthy charity. This assumption must have been placed in her mind by my saying that I had no permanent means of income, save what little money my father gave me. She appeared satisfied with my explanation but found it a bit odd that I 'dressed up' so much to please the tourists. The theme then turned to the male of the species and she wanted to know did I have a romantic commitment to someone? I relayed to her my heartache at losing my policeman friend, but not the real reason he had not been seen in Haworth of late.

"Poor you," sighed Joanna as she leant over the steering wheel of her car to peer out of the window.

"Do not fear," I smiled, "He will return to my arms yet!"

"You seem pretty sure?"

"I am, I know Mike... he will be back, you see."

"I wonder why he suddenly stopped seeing you. Had you had a lovers tiff?"

"No, certainly not."

"Look, you'll have to forgive me, but really, I find you are a little, shall we say, eccentric? I agree this is a famous place and literary shrine to genius, but normal girls don't go around every day like you, dressing up in period costume. What do your parents have to say about it?"

"My mother died when I was an infant, my father is very tolerable of the situation."

"What about your Mike?"

""He does not mind in the slightest."

"He must be a very understanding bloke, especially with him being a cop! Anyway, you know who I am, what is your name?"

"Charlotte," I smiled briefly.

"Oh, nice name," mused Joanna, her bright blue eyes looking me up and down, "Were you born in Haworth?"

"No, my original home is near Bradford." "Oh right. I won't prey any further, I'm sorry."

"Please do not apologise, Joanna, there is no need; I understand your concern for me and the mode of my dress, but really there is nothing sinister about me, I just like doing something that marks me out as different from all the other folk."

"I suppose you dress normal at home then, for your father?"

"Yes, of course," I lied.

Silence reigned for a moment as both of us stared out of the car windows at the glorious scenery of Sladen valley with Stanbury overlooking the wider expanse of Lower Laither Reservior. This drew comment and a deep sigh of resignation from my young friend.

"You are very lucky living out here, Charlotte. My home is in Manchester, in a dingy bedsit surrounded by noise and exhaust fumes. I'd give anything to be able to live up here."

"Cannot you purchase a property?" I suggested.

"One big problem – money!" Joanna answered ruefully.

"I fear it is not all romantic out here as you seem to think, my dear!" I laughed.

Joanna turned and gave me a quizzical look.

"You do talk strangely," she said.

"I do?"

"Yes, rather old English... quite refined in fact... are your family well off?"

"Ha!" I laughed out loudly. "I suspect we are not, my father was only on a very low income from the church."

"The church? Your father was a vicar?"

"That is correct, my dear."

"Is he now retired?"

"Very much so," I smiled, choosing my words carefully, I had begun another explosive situation before I'd realised.

"What about brothers and sisters?"

"All gone, I'm afraid."

"Married off, you mean?"

"No, Joanna, I remain the sole survivor of a very large family, all my siblings passed away through various forms of acute illness... mainly consumption."

"Oh gosh, how awful for you," sighed Joanna, briefly reaching out to pat my hand. "What about your father, is he still in reasonable health?"

"I fear that he too succumbed, many years ago."

"Oh? I got the impression he was still around?"

"I am sorry to inform you that I have none but myself to care for these days," I sighed heavily.

"Have you any other family, aunts or cousins?"

"None."

"Oh, Charlotte! What an awful life for you; now I can understand why you dress up the way you do, pretending to be a Victorian girl must give you a great boost and take your mind off things."

"I must confess it does help," I smiled.

"I live alone too, Charlotte, so I can see where you are coming from. But unlike you I have lots of friends and a good social life. How do you spend your evenings?"

"Usually I retire to my bedroom."

"What a life, perhaps I could call round and cheer you up one evening?"

"Oh, that will not be necessary," I hastily told her, alarm bells beginning to ring in my head. I had brought this situation on myself, now I would have to bluff my way out of it somehow. Then Joanna turned to Mike for her next batch of questions, firstly asking me if he has stayed the night with me! I thought that rather impertinent but I bit my tongue and answered truthfully, suggesting Mike had no desire as yet to become that involved with me.

"I don't know why you won't go into Keighley to look for him. After all, from what you have told me about him, you two seem very close. Maybe I could take you? I've nothing to rush home for."

"That is very good of you, my dear, but Mike may be out in the countryside driving his car on the lookout for felons."

"Felons?" frowned Joanna, turning to face me again with a quizzical look about her.

"I think you modern day people call them crooks?" I began, then to my dismay I realised what I had said!

"Modern? You're modern!" laughed Joanna, "Apart from your clothes that is! I think there is something mysterious about you Charlotte!"

"Oh? Why do you imply that?"

"Well, I mean, going around every day of your life, walking up and down Haworth's streets dressed in period costume just to please the tourists? Who is paying you to do it?"

"Paying me? I assure no one is bequeathing me money, I simply walk around because I love doing what I do."

"Do the tourists give you tips then? Or ask awkward questions?"

"No of course not, Joanna. They take me as they find me."

"I bet there are a few words said behind your back though?"

"By the by, that is their prerogative!" I scoffed.

"So where do you buy all your costumes from Charlotte?"

"I do not, I have had these garments for many years; I have a whole room full of different attire."

"Don't you ever fancy wearing jeans or short skirts sometimes?"

"To entrap young gentlemen you mean? I am afraid I am no splendid bird of paradise: men walk by me without a second glance. Whatever I dress myself in will not gain me one jot of beauty to my ugly face."

"Charlotte! You're not ugly, do you hear me? Stop putting yourself down and start living, girl!"

"I wish!" I laughed.

"Sorry?"

"The word 'living'"

"What about it?" frowned Joanna.

"Oh, nothing, please forgive me. I daresay I was being a little morbid."

"Yes you were Charlotte. If you want my advice, you will ditch your funny clothes and dress sexily to please your Mike."

"I am afraid you place too much importance on facial looks; is it not wise to concentrate on the inner person?"

"Yes, you are right, but that comes later. You have to attract the man first!"

"And you have achieved this amazing feat Joanna?!"

"Once or twice!" she chuckled, "at the minute though, there is no one special in my life."

"I think Mike would like the look of you."

"Charlotte! You shouldn't be saying such things!"

"Well if I cannot have him as my own it is better perhaps to convey him to someone who can make him happier."

"I'm not pinching your boyfriend!" cried Joanna, giving me a withering stare.

"You do not have to, my dear, Mike will make his own mind up if ever the pair of you shall meet."

"What, and you wouldn't feel jealous? Another girl chatting up your fella?"

"Perhaps a little, but I have had my time with him, I fear our relationship has run its course."

"If it were me, I'd get myself down to the police station and confront him... or do you have his home address?"

"No, but even if I did, I would not invade his privacy... there are complications you see."

"What sort of complications?"

"Oh, I should not have mentioned it, they are trivial."

"Why, are you trying to say that Mike is a married man?"

"I hope not! I laughed, "No sometimes it is very difficult for me to avail myself to Mike... we are on a different level at times."

"I'm sorry Charlotte, but you aren't talking much sense. Look, please forgive me, but are you really being straight with me? Some of these things don't add up."

"I do beg your pardon Joanna. But pray, where in my epistle have I misled you?"

"There you go again Charlotte, your strange way of talking. I must congratulate you on being a fine actress though, you play the part of a Victorian girl very well."

I tensed, Joanna was probing deeply. Already she was holding me in a critical gaze, I knew that I could not keep up with the pretence much longer, I had to escape.

"Forgive me, Joanna, but I feel I must depart from your hospitality now, I have taken up quite enough of your time already..."

"Charlotte – wait! – don't go!" she pleaded as I pushed open the car door. I felt her hand restrain me but I pleaded with her to let me go, which she finally did, albeit reluctantly.

"Take care then Charlotte. I might see you around, yes?"

"That would be most pleasing, my dear. Thank you," I smiled.

As I walked off, Joanna started her car and reversed out, then sounded her horn as she drove past me and away from Haworth. I had had a very lucky escape there, but what to do now that I was still visible to all? Worse still, a rather stout looking gentleman was walking towards me, leading a mongrel dog.

"Now then," he smiled thinly as I attempted to walk past him.

"Hello Sir," I smiled and meant to carry on walking.

"Hang on," he said gruffly, allowing his dog freedom to sniff at my clothes.

"Something wrong, Sir? Why do you wish to try and detain me?"

"Oh you're one of those bloody lah-de-dah women are you?" he scowled.

"I beg your pardon, Sir?"

"Why are you dressed up like that? Are you deranged or something?" he snapped.

I felt anger rising within me and my cheeks became uncomfortable warm.

"I wish to convey to you that how I choose to attire myself is no concern of yours, Sir!"

"What? You cheeky cow! Go on, **** off before I set my dog on you... I reckon you're a nutter!"

I was livid with the wretched person, and even though I was not acquainted with the foul language he was using on me I chose to keep silent and hurried off, his words of "You junkie!" filling my ears. The bald-headed fellow had distressed me deeply by his cold and unfriendly attitude and I swore revenge on him. I must escape!

Chapter Seventeen

"Ah! Young lady, a word please, if you don't mind?"

It was Mrs Carrington! I had walked back to the Parsonage with a view of entering by the front door, make some pretext to the ticket operative and then hide myself in the cellar until the place was locked up for the night. Unfortunately, as soon as I passed the gift shop window, an assistant alerted Mrs Carrington who immediately ran and detained me. We were outside in the garden area, and I had just been steeling myself to enter the museum under false pretences.

"What is it you wish to speak to me about?"

"Come to my office and you will find out, young lady!" she answered abruptly, holding my right arm and urging me up the stone steps to the front door. Both tourists and staff members alike gave me curious stares as Mrs Carrington half-walked, half-pushed me towards her office over the gift shop! I prayed that Martha Clayton would come to my aid, but I was sadly bereft of all help from that direction. I gritted my teeth ready to face the test of my life – or death – whichever you, the Reader, will prefer!

"Right!" she said, sternly, inviting me to be seated in a chair facing her. She looked over her dark rimmed spectacles at me and held me in a withering stare for a few moments. "I think it is time you explained yourself, young lady!"

"About what, if you please?" I asked, clenching my hands over my waist.

"You informed me that you belonged to a theatre group, a group I cannot trace! Can you throw any light on the subject?"

"I may have misled you at the time, Mrs Carrington, but you appeared quite unconcerned of my distress of having a man follow me."

"What man? We searched high and low for you, and found no one. And what is your relationship with the young police officer, Constable Gilmore?"

"Forgive me, dear lady, but I fail to see what business it is of yours, or anyone else's, what P.C Gilmore and I do together!"

"It *is* when it comes to the security of this valuable collection of Brontëana!" snapped Mrs Carrington, her face becoming quite flushed as her anger rose.

"What are you accusing me of?" I demanded.

Suddenly, before she could answer me, a powerful surge went through my whole frame. I heard Mrs Carrington scream but did not take heed, I was free again, invisible!

Poor Mrs Carrington! Medical assistance was called when they found her slumped over her desk, the ambulance crew suspecting a heart attack. I have to admit that I smiled with glee as they removed my tormentor from the Parsonage and sped her with all haste to Airedale Hospital in nearby Keighley. Once again, I had cheated fate, coming within a whisker of being unmasked. As for Mrs Carrington, once she had recovered from her trauma she was never seen again in Haworth and resigned from her post over the telephone. The Museum had no choice but to desperately look around for a competent successor.

***

Dear Reader, I was in turmoil. My whole existence – not my life, that was impossible, but my days of walking unseen amongst my fellow Haworthians and tourists alike – now seemed an impossibility. The moment I set foot beyond the safety of the Parsonage walls I ran the risk of the awful power that imprisoned me making me visible again. Sally Mitchell had sworn that Martha Clayton no longer had any interest in me; then why, pray, must she prolong my suffering in the world? On the one hand I wanted to be free to roam unseen through eternity, on the other, I yearned for the strong arms of my policeman. I could not have it both ways.

After the altercation on the moor with the man walking his dog, I was not so sure about living in the modern world anyway. He had treated me with total contempt and disrespect. At least he could have shown a little interest and seek further information on why I dress the way I do. Of course, I would never have professed who it was he facing, but I could have furnished him with a few untruths like myself appertaining to be an actress; I suspect then he would have gone on his way quite happily, and have a good reason to boast to his friends of whom he had encountered. Instead, he had chosen to treat me cruelly. And what of Mike? I suspect he had gone off the idea of courting me, not because of fear of losing his employment, but because he was generally convinced he was on the road to nowhere with me, which was true of course. Lately I suspected that for his sanity and peace of mind it would be best not to tempt fate by associating with me further. Both of us had sampled something new and different, quite removed from normality, but we had realised that our love for each other could never be. One instant I were a spirit, the next I were as wholesome as he but without time on my side. A difficult choice had to be taken, I had to break free of Martha's spell, but how and who could help me? The answer was to come even quicker than I could have ever hoped for!

Nothing untoward happened during the next week and I began to think that Martha really had tired of hurting me. I spoke with Sally and Adam on two occasions, and they assured me that there was no trace of the quarryman's wife. Maybe she really was at peace now, slumbering underneath her gravestone? I hardly dared to believe that she had at long last released her claws from me. It was a futile hope, dear Reader!

With everything now seemingly back to normal, I once again took up my silent wanderings of Haworth. It was on one such afternoon that I finally saw Mike again... and he had a young woman with him! I could hardly believe my eyes, and was a little more than angry to note that he appeared to be getting on quite well with her. He was stood leaning against his white and yellow police car, while she stood with arms folded, they were deep in conversation. I moved in closer, and to my surprise and astonishment, I saw it was Joanna! Heavens above! What had brought them together so abruptly, and what was she doing back in Haworth?

I felt quite vexed as I drew alongside the pair, who seemed to be finding something quite amusing. I listened in intently.

"So you've met my lady-friend have you?" grinned Mike.

"Yes, and I'm still not sure about her even though you say she is quite normal... I mean, walking about in Victorian clothes!"

"There's nothing sinister about her, she just loves dressing up, that's all."

"Some of the things she told me didn't add up though."

"Like what?"

"Well, for instance, Charlotte told me her Dad didn't mind her dressing up, then a few moments later she told me he had died ages ago!"

"She does tend to get a little confused," nodded Mike.

"Does she indeed!" I scowled.

"Anyway I'm glad we have met... I thought perhaps I might be in with a chance of seeing Charlotte's bloke – there aren't that many police cars in Haworth!"

"Lucky for you I swapped routes," grinned Mike, "I was shocked when you stopped me and asked me if I knew Charlotte though!"

"Yes, I'm sorry to have rushed out and waved you down like that, but I had to know if it was you or not, or if you could pass a message on to Mike."

"Pretty resourceful, aren't you?"

"Yes Mike, when I make up my mind about something, I try and carry it through."

"A lady after my own heart!"

"Never mind me... when are you going to see Charlotte again?"

"I don't know, it's becoming increasingly difficult. And what with my boss altering my patrol..."

"That's a poor excuse Mike. What about when you're not working?"

"I usually go out with mates, to clubs or whatever."

"And meet other women?"

"Sometimes... anyway, what's with the lecture? I am a single bloke y'know."

"But what about Charlotte? It was obvious to me that she has deep feelings for you."

"Oh aye, what did she say?"

"The usual stuff about commitment and being in love... like any normal girl would be."

"I'm afraid Charlotte is far from normal, Joanna!" Mike suddenly blurted out. This immediately put me on edge, wondering what he would issue forth regarding my person. I had a good reason to feel anxious!

"Charlotte isn't normal?" questioned Joanna, "That's a bit harsh isn't it?"

Mike looked down at the ground, his face unsmiling and tense.

"What is it Mike? What are you keeping from me?"

"You wouldn't believe me if I told you," he said, without looking up, "Charlotte is different in a way you could never come to terms with."

"Well, I agree that her dress sense leaves a lot to be desired, but if it makes her happy to go about like that, where's the harm in it? I bet most of the shopkeepers and B&B's in the village welcome her contribution."

"If that were the case, Joanna, it would be fine, but the fact is hardly anyone has ever seen her walking up and down."

"Rubbish!" exclaimed Joanna in a fit of mirth, "You can't very well miss her when she's dressed like that!"

"If she were a real person?"

"What?" exclaimed Joanna, her smile vanishing. I too became apprehensive, for this was the moment I had long dreaded, the moment of truth.

"I think you had better sit in my car a moment, Joanna; what I'm going to tell you defies all logic, and I won't be offended and arrest you if you call me a liar!"

I watched the pair of them as they settled down in the warmth and privacy of the patrol car. I did not join them, I had no need to. I watched in cold trepidation the look on poor Joanna's pretty face as the gruesome account unfolded. Much to my astonishment, when finally Mike allowed her to go Joanna did not smile or wave as he drove off; instead she sank onto a park bench looking shocked and bewildered. I wanted to go to her and hug her tightly, but I had not the power. Martha Clayton had denied me the basic instinct of humanity.

After a while of deep contemplation, my young Miss rose to her feet and started to walk back up Main Street, still deep in thought. If only I could be made real again, with just enough time to offer an explanation and to reassure my young friend.

Chapter Eighteen

It was a very long time before I acquainted myself with Mike or Joanna; indeed, late autumn was upon us and the streets of Haworth cold and windswept. The summer's visitors had long gone and only the foolhardy remained to sample our inhospitable climate.

My existence had been largely barren of late, not even my sister Emily making an appearance – it was as if the moor had swallowed her up. I am glad to report, though, that the Parsonage's exorcism had been a dismal failure and I was free to wander from room to room as I pleased. There is a lot to be explained about the so-called 'holy water' clergymen are want to splash over a haunted room! I had no intention of vacating my former home on the whim of some excitable man of the cloth; normality had indeed returned the moment the deranged gentleman left the building! To keep the peace and not frighten the staff, I kept well out of their way at all times. To all, the exorcism had proven a great success. I wanted it to remain so! To ease my boredom, I went in search of Martha Clayton and Sally Mitchell. At first, I suffered many days of impatience, my quarry refusing to show itself. And then, one day in desperation, I thought of the old stone workings up on Penistone Hill. In all haste I repaired there, convinced that was where Martha must be found: it was the place of her husband's demise, or at least, the site of the accident leading to it. The moment I topped the steep hill and looked down into the former quarry workings, I was proven correct. There, far below, sat a figure dressed in mourning black, hunched over a large boulder that had at some stage been torn from its resting place on the valley walls. I approached Martha with some trepidation, fearing what she would bestow upon me next. However, she was not aware of me until the very last moment, as I made my way off the hillside and over the flat ground of the quarry bottom.

"What d'you want?" she asked gruffly as I stood before her.

"If you please, Madam, I would fall upon your mercy to release me from the spell in which you have placed me."

"Why? I thought you liked your young man, Miss Brontë?"

"I do, but it is of no use. We can never be happy together, and you know it, Martha."

"Pray, why ever not, child?" frowned the old woman.

"When you conceived your plan for me, had you not taken into account that your power lasts only hours? What kind of a situation is that for a gentleman to tolerate? I go in and out of his life like a Will O' the Wisp!"

"You ought to be grateful that I allow you moments of pleasure at all, Miss Brontë... You indeed did not have much in your original life with Bell-Nicholls."

"You have no idea what my husband and I shared!" I accused the grinning woman.

"It is of no consequence Madam, I have witnessed the young man you think so highly of and he is a good catch... but not to be yours unless you are prepared to surrender your soul totally to me."

"Never!" I cried out, every fibre of my body rebelling against this awful woman.

"Very well," she sneered, getting to her feet, "Someone else already has him under her power anyway!"

"Who?" I demanded, knowing full well the old crone was referring to Joanna.

"A young lady from t'other side of the Pennines, a right bonny Lancashire lass!"

"You are telling me old news, Martha Clayton. Miss Joanna is my good friend on earth."

"Is she now, Miss Brontë? Well, pray let me inform you that she has ideas of her own concerning the young man. And she is living – you are not!"

"If it has to be, then I accept it," I retorted, my cheeks burning.

"And you are not a little jealous, Miss Brontë?"

"What is the point? As you admirably mentioned, I have no power to be permanently placed beside the man I love."

"I could give you that power, Miss Brontë, if you will renounce God."

"Why? Why? You old witch!" I cried, stooping to pick up a stone and hurling it at the grinning woman. Of course it passed harmlessly through her head.

"If it is the last thing I do, I will have you exorcised, Martha Clayton!" I cried out, turning on my heel.

"Your threats mean nothing to me lass, you have no power now to contact any human. Once more you are doomed forever to roam this land... unless you change your mind."

***

The enormity of the toothless old woman's words stung me like a wasp as I made my way down the walled-in track towards St. Michael's churchyard. Now I really was in desperate straits: with no hope of materialising before either Mike or Joanna, I was once again a prisoner of death! Yes, I would be free to roam my beloved Haworth once more, to mingle with the tourists and locals alike, but at what cost? In one fell swoop I had lost the love of my young man, the patient listener to all my woes. Even worse, I had lost my new friend Joanna.

That fateful morning as I walked through the foggy gloom down the lane by St Michael's I was not to know that salvation was near to hand. I had risen from my slumbers with yet another excruciating headache which was made worse by looking out of the lattice at the stark burial ground with its skeletal trees and dank gravestones. Even in the brightest summer, the cemetery gives off an air of deep foreboding; in winter, it is doubly so.

The time was a little after eleven when I ventured out unseen into the cold still air. Apart from a gentleman placing a billboard outside the King's Arms proclaiming the day's menu, not another soul broke the stillness. I made haste to reach the church steps, intending to once more make the journey out to Martha Clayton's old cottage up at Marsh. Despite what you, Reader, have been told about spirits and their lightening-like movements, it is not so, we still walk or run at the same pace as you, the fortunate living! It would take me just as long to reach my destination as in real life. Today, however, my plans would be thwarted the moment I passed the Villette Coffee House. I espied in there one Marie McKuskey! She sat alone by the window, staring outside. No other persons, save the staff, occupied the cafe. I decided to visit the woman and observe her at close quarters.

Mrs McKuskey did not stir as I placed myself discreetly opposite her, she was deep in thought. I noticed a piece of writing paper by her fingers and she looked very sad. With a certain amount of bravado, I rose and walked around to her side of the table and quite cheekily read the contents of the few lines thereon! It proclaimed that her affair with her English gentleman had been terminated by him, that his wife had learnt of the illicit union and challenged him to decide who he really wanted to be with. Like the coward he was, he went crawling back, begging for the forgiveness of his legal spouse. Mrs McKuskey looked like the typical mistress of rejection. I knew how she felt, as I had suffered the same feelings at the hands of M'sieur Heger and lately, it seems, of Mike. I indeed felt sorry for her, but at the same time I thought she must have entered into the affair with eyes wide open, knowing full well that they would be discovered. What event had brought about the end of their relationship, I did not know, but what interested me more was what was she doing back in Haworth? I noticed the note was dated back to August; five months of heartache and loneliness had been this wretched woman's companion. Was she here to revive and relive old memories, or had she come back on business to complete the book she claimed to be writing? Very soon, I gained an answer. I had barely returned to my seat when in walked Joanna, making straight for Mrs McKuskey!

I sat there, open-mouthed, as Mrs McKuskey rose briefly to greet her young companion. Her sad features of a moment past had now gone and she was smiling broadly.

"Glad you could make it, honey," she said, "So what have you got to tell me?"

"Not a lot," shrugged Joanna. "I've spoken to Mike, though."

"And?"

"He hasn't seen her for ages now."

"Damn! D'you reckon she's high-tailed it back to her vault?"

"I don't know... who is to say?"

"Have you completed your story about the girl then?"

"Almost, Marie, but it would be nice to pen a happy ending, I hate leaving over loose ends!"

"Well if she won't contact Mike anymore, there isn't a Goddamned lot we can do about it honey. Have you researched the Clayton woman?"

"Yes I've been to the archive office in Keighley, everything Charlotte told me rang true."

"And the Mitchell case?"

"Yep... all true."

"Doggone it Joanna, I can't believe we are having this screwy conversation. How do you figure she is able to keep crossing over from one dimension to the other?"

"Charlotte claims it is all down to the spell the Clayton woman put on her."

"Honey! Be realistic here – no magician is that good! It is beyond all imagination that a dead person can come back to life and walk amongst us, only to vanish into the spirit world until the next time."

"Yes, Marie, I totally agree with you... but somehow it has happened, and to a famous person at that!"

"I hope you have kept this story to yourself?"

"You bet!" laughed Joanna.

"I really didn't believe Mike when he took me to one side and told me the story, I thought he was nuts... I thought both of you were nuts!"

"Common reaction, Marie!"

"So, your story? You are changing the names I take it?"

"Absolutely, I don't want suing by someone if I claimed I was really writing a true story concerning Charlotte Brontë!"

"You reckon she also mentioned her sister Emily? Something about Mike coming face to face with her too?"

"Yes that's right. They were sat in Mike's police car on Penistone Hill one day, just chatting."

"Hell, it sounds incredible! Charlotte Brontë sat in a cop car? The mind boggles!"

"If it wasn't such a serious situation it would be laughable!"

"Too true, honey! Anyway, what is your next move?"

"I thought I might go the whole hog and get photographic evidence?"

"Great idea, Joanna, I never thought of that one."

"All I have to do is get Charlotte's agreement."

"When do you figure on seeing her again?"

"How long is a piece of string?" giggled Joanna, totally unaware that the object of her amusement was sitting right next to her!

"Is there any way you could persuade Charlotte to appear to you?"

"No, Marie. I'm afraid it's all down to chance: she could come back now, tomorrow, perhaps never. Who knows?"

"What was your reaction the first time it happened?"

"Nothing, I didn't witness her appearing. I dropped my pen and clipboard by the church steps, then suddenly she was there helping me to retrieve them."

"I'd love to see her suddenly materialise out of thin air!" Marie said ruefully. Reader, if it were possible I would have granted her that wish! As it was, Mrs McKuskey had no idea that I was seated within touching distance of her, her powers of detection taking a well-earned rest I daresay!

Chapter Nineteen

I left the Villette cafe deep in thought, Joanna's plan to take photographs of me sent a chill through my being. On the one hand I would have loved to show the world that there is another life beyond the bounds of earth, but common sense told me it was not the sort of employment I should be entering into. Up until now, folks in and around Haworth were, to a greater extent, not aware of my comings and goings as a free spirit. To suddenly produce pictures of me would be like placing me in a freak show. I knew for certain that no one in their right mind would believe who I really was, yet doubtless I did not want to become the butt of scorn and ridicule. Joanna and Marie would fare no better, people accusing them of either having wild imaginations or creating a person said to be the reincarnation of the deceased, for monetary gain. I wanted no part of it, but at the same time I wished to be free of my prison and the clutches of Martha Clayton. I also realised that there was no hope for me now as regards Mike; already, I fancy, he had set his hat on Joanna. It was only natural, she being quite a handsome and bubbly young lady. She had all the qualities going for her that men were looking for, and Mike was no exception.

It was a sad day indeed for me, because I knew that I was losing the man I had fallen in love with. But what chance had I of gaining his love on a permanent holding, when I was only a mere spirit? Only the witchcraft of Martha Clayton gave me precious moments with him; there was no possibility of ever being by his side until his life's end. I had been born, married, and died, as is the way of our Lord. Somehow, I had been reinstated to life by that atrocious woman only to be snatched away again at her behest. I could never marry Mike nor bear his children; I was a figure of little substance, a phantom, a ghost, whatever. Without Martha's intervention, I would have remained so, and no one would have been any the wiser. Unfortunately, I now found myself the victim of one of the seven deadly sins. I had fallen deeply in love!

***

I felt so helpless and heartbroken as I slowly walked around my old village, I felt bereft of friendship in the spirit world. Not even my dear Emily had put in an appearance of late; it seemed that I was the solitary survivor left out of a multitude of lost souls. I believe I may have been far better off to let that reverend exorcise me and allow me free passage to my burial place, there to remain silent forever and trouble no one.

However, these circumstances had already befallen me, and I would have to endure the situation however long it must take. I even thought of visiting the church and earnestly ask for the Lord's help and guidance in this matter, but I could not, I was dead and no prayers could do me any good now. No, the only solution would be to go on in my journey and sit out the storm until my Lord decided enough was enough and He would put an end to my suffering.

My mind went back to those happy moments Mike and I shared together in that old barn. Intimacy was as good as I ever dared to hope; the act of physical love was overpowering my senses and leading me into a wave of ecstasy. I did not feel the revulsion at what I had allowed Mike to do to me: we were just like any other loving couple, committing our bodies to each other. And afterwards, we skipped, danced and laughed our way over the field like a couple of teenage schoolchildren who had just done something naughty. I cannot imagine Papa's facial expression though, had he witnessed my wrong doings with Mike! Yes, Reader, in the eyes of God it was wrong for me to allow my earthly feelings get the better of me. When a person dies and is selected by our Lord to be a true and trusted spirit, he or she is expected to behave in a way that is above degeneration and temptation; I believe I had angered my Maker and He was punishing me accordingly. Now everything was gone and all hope for a happy future with my young gentleman dashed to pieces. My only way out now was to elicit my escape back to the other, safer, world of the undead. While I was free to roam wherever I pleased I was harming no one; all that needed to be done now, most earnestly, was to find some means of achieving my goal and bidding goodbye to the real world. I had enjoyed my brief hours of liberation, now I must return from whence I came.

Sadness dogged my footsteps as I sought refuge inside St. Michael's Church. I was not alone, there were quite a number of folk wandering up and down the aisles admiring the rich interior of the church. They did not heed my progress as I walked amongst them and found myself a seat by the chancel steps. The rear windows filled my vision, depicting Christ and his disciples seated for the Last Supper. I called out to my Lord to help me, I knew no other from whom I could successfully plead for help. Whether my prayers were answered, I know not, as only the steady hum of gas fires touched my hearing. Eventually I rose and left the church, my mind deep in thought. As I reached the door a light flashed above my head from the giant window at the tower end of the church. I thought nothing of it as I emerged into the daylight.

Suddenly I felt someone take my right arm and call out my name with a voice full of joy and excitement. I spun around and beheld Joanna and Mrs McKuskey, the latter of whom had both hands covering her mouth, her eyes wide with fear.

"Upon my soul! Can you see me, Joanna?" I exclaimed, my body suddenly going very shaky.

"Of course I can! Oh, Charlotte, this is wonderful. Marie and I had been talking about you not so many minutes ago!"

"Yes, child, I am well aware of that," I smiled briefly.

"You were?" frowned the American woman, suddenly finding her voice.

"Yes Madam, I occupied a seat opposite you in the Villette cafe. I heard every word you uttered about me and Mike."

I thought Marie was going to faint on the spot, her face went deathly pale at my announcement. In fact both ladies were indeed very shocked.

"So? Now you can see me, what are your plans for me?"

"Plans? We have no plans, Charlotte."

"Please, young lady, do me the honour of permitting myself to have some intelligence, I heard you mention you would be most gratified to take photographs of me, is not that so?"

"Well, yes, that's right... if you don't mind?"

"Forgive me, Joanna, but I do indeed mind. I refuse to take part in your wild idea, it is not right."

"Why not?"

"Because, my dear, you would be altering history and you would bring down all sorts of problems on your young head. In any case, no one would be prepared to believe you."

"How could they not, if your face was there for all to see?" cut in Mrs McKuskey.

"I will not allow you to dishonour either yourselves or me. Let the past stay where it is, no good will come of your whimsical ideas... or do you just want to make a fortune out of me?"

"No I do not, Charlotte!" exclaimed Joanna, tugging my arm again.

"Then, pray, what are your motives?"

"All I wish is to get a good story going."

"You can do that without my help, Joanna,"

"Maybe so... but I would change your name anyway, no one would stop to think it was Charlotte Brontë I was using as my story piece."

"Cut the crap, honey," scoffed Marie, "Even the dumbest jerk would recognise the Brontë face!"

"Well thanks very much!" cried Joanna, angrily turning on her companion.

"Shush now," I said, coming between the quarrelsome pair.

"I have informed you of my decision, Joanna, so do me a great service and turn your thoughts to someone else less well-known, if you please!"

Joanna fell silent and folded her arms, a disdainful look clouding her normally cheerful face. She would have to accept what I told her: I was adamant that I should not re-emerge as a heroine for a modern tale and that my picture must not be used to promote the work, regardless of however good it may or may not be in the eyes of the readers.

"Tell me something..." said Marie, breaking the awkward silence, "Why do you keep on appearing and vanishing... are you playing some sort of game here?"

"I only wish it were that simple, Madam!" I replied coldly, "I am held in the power of someone who is the daughter of Satan; I earnestly wish someone may deliver me from the spell so that I may return to my own world."

"Joanna can!"

"What?" I exclaimed.

"Sure she can, honey. Joanna dabbles in that sort of thing, don't you?"

"It may not be the sort of thing that Charlotte is pinning her hopes on though," smiled Joanna.

"Mercy me, child, what is it you refer to... exorcism?"

"No, not that... just making lost souls happy, I guess. I pray for them and ask God to return them to their former life."

"But how can that be so, they are dead, are they not?"

"I suppose so... but if I explain to them that they ought to be walking unseen in their own day, instead of now in the modern world, then they ought to be happy with that. Don't you agree Charlotte?"

"Not really. I would sooner explore unseen in today's world. I have no time for the 1850s I already know all there is to know about that era, it is the future which interests me more."

"What about your family though? Would they not want you to return to their time?"

"I doubt whether my siblings would agree with you Joanna, most, if not all of them, roam about Haworth now in the modern time. Your plan would not make a farthing of difference."

"Oh? I wasn't aware that the rest of your family members are prone to wandering from their graves?"

"My dear! When a person dies, his or her soul is released for all time... why there are literally tens of thousands walking unseen even now on the streets and alleys of this dark and sad village!"

Both ladies looked absolutely shocked at my disclosures, but it was best that they learnt the truth, and that I were not the only spirit roaming abroad.

"It sends shivers through me... thinking of all those ghoulish people walking amongst us!" exclaimed Joanna.

"They are not ghouls, my dear, just ordinary folk who have passed away with little pretensions to fame or glory. Most of the men were common mill workers or quarry men, but they were no less important to God than you or I. We are what we make of ourselves, but in death we are all equal."

"I suppose so, but it still gives me the creeps to know that I am being watched by hundreds of pairs of eyes!"

"Haworth is not unique my dear, all over the country, indeed all over the world, spirits of the dead roam at will; as you are a part of life, so they are of death and the afterlife. Only in extreme cases do the dead appear to be living. Folk go about their business totally unaware of the fact."

"And you are one of a small minority then?"

"I swear I did not wish it to be so, Joanna, I was quite happy to wander unseen."

"And now... I take it you would love to hold onto Mike if it were possible?"

"Yes Joanna, but I fear it is not; I am a victim of evil, and the sooner the source of that evil is destroyed, the better. Then I can bid you a fond farewell."

"You tell us that now Charlotte, but I suspect you would really miss this modern world?"

"Perhaps, but somehow I would not be too concerned, after all I would still be walking amongst you all, just like my fellow spirits."

"Absolutely, but you would be unable to feel, touch, or love Mike as you once did."

"My love has not cooled for him, Joanna, but I cannot go on as I am, I need release!"

"Maybe Marie can help you there?"

"How?" I said, turning to look at her dumb-struck companion.

"Marie does exorcism... she could nail down Martha Clayton for you and refuse her leave from her burial place."

"Good heavens, child! You mean the very help I so earnestly seek can be achieved by this lady?"

"That's right, honey," the American spoke at last. "It all depends on you though, what do you want?"

"I do beg of your pardon, Madam, but what do you refer to exactly?"

"Do you really want to go back? Or stay here with your cop boyfriend? If I perform an exorcism on that broad you despise, the spell could swing either way... you may end up a prisoner of our world, unable to return to the afterlife."

I was truly shocked by that statement, dear Reader; I had not given it a moment's thought, naturally believing Martha's hold on me would perish the moment she went to the grave. I told the two ladies that my mind was in turmoil.

"It's make your mind up time, honey. Do you still love this Mike guy?"

"Of course I do... and yet? I do not think I could face life in a totally alien world."

"Think of the benefits Charlotte!" encouraged Joanna, gripping my arm again, "You would be free unconditionally, free to go wherever you please. And besides, if you married and wanted to become a housewife there are all sorts of modern gadgets that are there at your disposal to make life easier."

"I like the idea of matrimony," I smiled.

"Well then, Charlotte?"

"No, child. I am afraid I would not be capable of fitting in to your modern world, and at the back of my mind would be the constant fear of the afterlife. It is true that I would be extremely happy with Mike, but it cannot be... the Lord would never allow the union."

"He hasn't stopped you so far," Joanna reminded me.

"Indeed, but He has had no part in my journey to your world. No, my dear, I think it would be best if I lay down all my hopes and dreams and repair back to my spirit world. I am happy there, and I know of no other place I would rather be."

"You are very sad, do you know that?" Joanna said, releasing her grip on me, "You have a chance of untold happiness and love, yet you turn your back on it."

"That is not how I view it, my dear: I have stayed in your modern world far too long, it is now time for me to return to a place of safety. I have seen many things of this age that I do not like, indeed, the attitude of some fellows to others is quite appalling. It would seem everyone is against each other in some form or other; people are never as friendly as in my day. We had a strong sense of community and shared each other's hardships and problems. In your world it is every person for themselves."

"I find that hard to believe, Charlotte. You and your family led a life away from the people of Haworth. You were never allowed to mix with the other inhabitants!"

"Only while we were yet children," I corrected her.

"But you had few friends in Haworth... or so the history books tell us?"

"Pah! Believe what you will, Joanna. Books are made by people, they either add or subtract to make the work sound interesting. Why, we had many friends from the village, even folk from the mills. When I ran my Sunday school I made friendly acquaintance with many young parents."

"It doesn't say that," argued Joanna.

"By the by, my dear. All this mistrust and accusations against my integrity is not helping me solve the terrible situation I find myself in."

"Well, like I said, the offer is still there Charlotte. But if you really feel it is time you went back to your own world..."

"At this precise moment, Joanna, I do not know what I want. My heart is torn between two evils: to return to normality, or surrender myself to your modern world. Either way would not gain me true happiness, I am certain of it."

"Not even with Mike by your side?"

"Mike has eyes only for you now, Joanna dearest. I watched him keenly while you were in his company, it is the look of love I assure you."

"Rubbish!" laughed Joanna, "Mike and I hardly know each other and I was only concerned for your sake."

"Yes, very admirable, but how do you feel about him?"

"He's alright to talk to... unlike most policemen. I guess I felt quite relaxed in his company, but that is no reason to steal someone else's boyfriend."

"You would not be stealing him from me, I cannot own him like you would be able to do."

"You could if you let Marie and I help you Charlotte. It would be a simple matter of finding clothes for you and maybe lodging at Mike's until we could find you a proper home."

"Upon my soul child, I could never allow myself to live under the same roof as a gentleman until I were betrothed to him!" I cried out.

"Come off it Charlotte, what's the problem here? Mike has already admitted to me that you and he are more than just good friends."

"Oh my God!" I screeched, "What power has taken over his brain? I feel quite vexed that he should share our private life with a complete stranger!"

"Don't worry Charlotte, he didn't go into detail... he just left me with the impression that you and he were... y'know?"

I felt my cheeks colouring greatly; this man had abused my trust. Heaven help me if the American woman, who was now stood silently and listening to every word, took it upon herself to repeat my love affair in much greater detail. In that moment I knew there was nothing left but to escape back to my own time, the shame of what I had done was biting deeply into my conscience. Maybe to the other two ladies it was normal to talk freely about their male conquests but to a God-fearing staid Victorian like myself it was unforgiveable! I decided to wrench myself free of them, and, after offering apologies I hurried up the lane back to the Parsonage. However, even this plan failed me as soon as I mounted the steps by the front door. A stern-faced woman wearing spectacles arrested any further progress by demanding to know who I was and where I thought I was going without paying for a ticket!

"I do not need to purchase a ticket off you, Madam. This is my former home!" I cried out, trying to get past her. She resolutely stood in my way and threatened to call the police if I did not remove myself forthwith.

"People like you – dressed up as you are – ought to be ashamed of themselves, trying to make out that you're some famous person! You have a nerve if you think that by wearing Victorian garments you can get in here free of charge. Mrs Carrington alerted us some time ago to woman going about dressed and telling everyone she was a Brontë sister!"

"Madam, I am! I exclaimed.

"Yes, and I'm the Queen... now clear off before I have you arrested!"

I fumed and shouted at the stubborn woman but it made no difference, she was determined I would not enter the museum. I declared it was she who ought to seek medical help, and so enraging her even more! I suddenly found myself being pushed back down the entrance steps and the stout door shut in my face! I was livid! My own home and I was prevented from entering! Well, needs must, I would sally forth and enter by the gift shop, the woman could not be in two places at once!

I had not taken into account the sheer audacity of the wretched woman: she had watched my departure with grim satisfaction, but at once anticipated I would try to gain entry by some other means. Consequently, as soon as I pushed open the gift shop entrance door, I found my way barred by two other female staff. They made it quite clear that I was not welcome there and that any attempt an entry would be met by a robust defence! Glaring at them angrily, I had no choice but to retreat forthwith and eventually rejoin my two fellow companions who had eagerly followed me up to the Parsonage. The American woman seemed to find the whole situation quite amusing as I seethed and made clear my thoughts on not being allowed into my own home!

"You can't really blame the staff, Charlotte," smiled Joanna, placing a protective arm around my waist.

"Why am I not allowed to enter my old home? I mean no harm to anyone!" I cried, my cheeks burning in frustration.

"For all they know, you could be someone escaped from a mental hospital, Charlotte!"

"Why in heaven's name would they think that?"

"Well, the way you are dressed, for one thing... there can't be too many girls going around Haworth claiming they are the real Charlotte Brontë!"

"I uttered no such thing!"

"Maybe you didn't, Charlotte, but trying to force your way into the Parsonage wouldn't go down well either!"

"It *is* my old home! I am entitled to go where I please."

"Not in this life. Wait until you're invisible again."

"And pray, do you have any idea when that will be?" I answered scathingly.

"It's just a case of being patient," said Joanna, releasing her hand from me.

"Then kindly inform me what I must do in the meantime?"

"Come back with us to Villette, I'll get you a coffee and something to eat."

"Do not talk nonsense, child! I am incapable of swallowing victuals, you seem to forget that I am a mere spirit!"

"Not at the moment you're not!" argued my young companion.

"I will accept your invitation, but I warn you, it will only serve to cause you both deep embarrassment when I walk in there dressed as I am!"

"We'll take that risk, honey," laughed Marie, urging me forward by linking arms with me. Thankfully, dear Reader, I was to be spared that acute embarrassment the moment we ascended the step leading into the crowded cafe.

"Just a moment, young lady! We'd like a word with you down at the station," came a gruff male voice from behind us.

We all turned to face a burly police officer who was stood with a young lady of the law.

"I beg your pardon?" I snapped.

"Have you been causing trouble up at the museum?"

"Indeed I have not, so please leave me be and go about your other duties!" I ordered the sallow-looking officer. He was far from impressed as he let it be known that he was arresting me on charges of harassing the Parsonage staff!

"We were on our way up there, but you've saved us the bother," he growled, both officers gripping me tightly and half dragging me over the road to their car. I cried and yelled at them, but to no avail, and to add to my misery I found myself wearing unyielding handcuffs. I could never forget the embarrassment of that moment, as crowds of sight-seers looked on at my predicament. Joanna and Marie were helpless to do anything for me, they simply stood there in mute shock as I was driven off to Keighley. Thankfully my ordeal was nearing a swift conclusion, but for the officers in the car, well, their ordeal was just beginning.

The two of them took it in turns to question me as we ascended the steep hill of Lees, then turned left for the long descent into Keighley. As I once foretold, we spirit forms were never permitted to stray further than the immediate vicinity of our demise on earth. No sooner had we begun the downward drive than I felt a tremendous power surge through me. There came the clatter of metal as my earthly body freed itself of the manacles and I was no more. The poor police driver almost lost control of his car as he saw me vaporise in his mirror, his female companion making a most hideous scream. I was free!

Chapter Twenty

I could not imagine the furore I caused after I had removed myself from the clutches of the police. At first, they tried to cover themselves by claiming I was violently sick in their car and they made me get out whilst they cleaned up, and then in so doing I escaped before they realised what was going on. Of course, they might have got away with it had not the local press become involved in the story. As many pairs of eyes had watched my being arrested, it was inevitable that someone should go running to the newspapers when nothing had been heard of me since. It seemed that everyone wanted to know what had become of the 'little lady of Haworth'. The two police officers were put on the spot by their supervisors who had demanded a full explanation. When this was given in great nervousness they were almost dismissed from their employment, had it not been for Mike intervening on their behalf and then contacting both Marie McKuskey and Mrs Carrington. That did it! I would appear in the newspaper and on the TV and radio as various media companies descended on our village all eager to lay claim to be the first ones to catch sight of the 'ghost'. In an instant, I became a most wanted person, I felt as though I were a prisoner on the run!

I only became aware of this sad state of affairs as I silently mingled with the crowds on Main Street one day and noticed a gentleman reading a paper. I quietly edged close to him in the hope I may gain information about my reckless actions at the Parsonage. To my horror, it was much worse than I had feared, there in stark headlines, it read: 'Brontë Ghost Runs Rings Round Police'! As I read, my heart missed several beats. I felt intensely vulnerable and without hope of rescue. Joanna and Marie had seemingly vanished from the streets of Haworth, they had probably fled back to their respective homes in case the police accused them of something quite serious. Mike was not to be seen either; in the days and weeks ahead I felt forlorn and rejected.

***

Very soon another full year had passed. It was now late March, and the hawthorn in the fields and hedgerows were full of their pinky-white blossom. Spring was on its way in the Worth Valley, but it did nothing to lift my flagging spirits. All whom I had known and called my friends were nowhere to be seen. I had long since resumed my unseen walks around Haworth, visiting the church and Parsonage, taking brief sojourns on the nearby moorland. One good thing that came out of this loneliness was that the invisible power that had previously possessed me on several occasions, thrusting me backwards and forwards into the future, was no longer in evidence. For well nigh more than a year I had been free of the wretched Martha Clayton. Whether or not Marie McKuskey had carried out her word and exorcised the old woman back into her grave, I knew not. It felt wonderful to be free of the privations she had put me through, and I thanked my Lord for his great mercy. Sadly though, He did not intervene in the healing of my mind, a mind that was still resolutely yearning for Mike. Although I was indeed grateful for my newfound freedom, I nonetheless ached for the strong arms of my young gentleman and his touch on my bare skin. Once more, my thoughts returned to our act of intimacy together, when I had allowed him to enter my body in the act of physical union. Although the experience was brief it had sent me into a world of pleasurable ecstasy and had me crying out and gasping for breath. I had never known such deep satisfaction and enjoyment from a man making love to me. I craved more: he had ignited a spark within me, the flames of unbridled passion; a love totally subdued by moralistic constraints in my own time and day when the world of sex was non-existent and love only a product of fairy stories. I was once starved of physical love, but now Mike had unlocked my heart and shown me what real love was.

The more that I craved Mike's love, the worse I became. I realised I had been a fool to refuse the help of Joanna, if she again wished me to stay in the 21st century I would not hesitate; I would become Mike's wife and we would be forever happy. If only! Now I was once more trapped in the clutches of death. Once I had yearned to escape from the real world that Joanna knew, but now I earnestly wished to go back there. Yet without Joanna and Mrs McKuskey's help, it was a forlorn hope.

And so it was that Easter time came upon the village, with the special service within the church to remember Christ's crucifixion and His resurrection from the dead. As a child, my sisters and I loved Palm Sunday and especially the Easter cake that Tabby Ackroyd would bake for us! It was similar to a Christmas cake but daintily iced and trimmed differently, and we ate it with relish! Now, all I had were sweet memories of my childhood. At least I could join in the church service unseen. Like the Christmas carol service, the Easter one was well attended by local folk, with palm crosses given out to the children. I loved every moment of it as I sat right at the back of the church watching the proceedings.

Strangely, mine was the only empty pew. And then quite out of the blue, a bizarre occurrence took place, shocking me rigid! I had previously noticed a quite pretty but troublesome little girl running up and down the main aisle, her frustrated mother vainly trying to catch and control her offspring. This had happened several times with the mother eventually threatening to remove the child from church in order to bring calm – all whilst the hapless vicar was trying to preach his sermon from the pulpit! Suddenly, the youngster once again escaped her mother and ran squealing down the aisle towards me! I froze as the giggling little girl slumped down against the back of the pew and looked at me with her lovely hazel eyes.

"My Mummy likes chasing me!" she smiled, wriggling about in her seat.

"Caroline!" cried her exasperated mother, "Get over here at once! I've had enough of your antics showing me up, you're going outside!"

"Don't want to! I'm talking to the lady," she scowled.

"What are you talking about, you little devil?"

"This lady is smiling at me. She's wearing funny clothes!"

"Nonsense, there's no one there, now come on!"

"No! I won't... tell Mummy off, lady!" demanded the little girl.

"I'm afraid your dear mother is right, Miss Caroline, you must do as you are told."

"Mummy! Mummy! This lady called me Miss Caroline!" cried the child. She looked no more than five years of age and was dressed prettily in a pink chiffon dress that nicely became her young years. Her mother, however, was having none of it and passed straight through me to reach for her misbehaving child. This drew a howl of protest from Caroline!

"Mummy! You trod all over that lady, you might have hurt her!" As this was going on a churchwarden with a grim look on his face tried to get both Mother and daughter to leave. Caroline ran around the pew and back to me.

"What's your name, lady? Will you help me?" she cried, her hands trying to grab at my neck.

"My name is Charlotte, but I fear I cannot help you. You must do as your mother says."

"No!" screamed the youngster, evading capture once more, "Charlotte says I am naughty as well, I hate all of you!" cried Caroline.

"Charlotte?" frowned her mother, stopping dead in her tracks.

"Yes Mummy, the lady sat here in the long dress! She said I had to do what you tell me."

Suddenly, you could hear a pin drop in the church as the vicar was removing himself from his pulpit and hurrying towards us. I was mortified! How on earth could the child see me when others could not?

"Now then, young lady," smiled the vicar as he reached forwards to pat the child on the head, "Perhaps your Mummy will give you a sweet if you promise to be quiet until I've finished my sermon? After that you can run around again while we sing hymns, because no one will mind then!"

"I want to go home!" sulked Caroline, pursing her lips.

"Okay, if that is what you wish, I am sure that Mum would be happy to take you."

"What about Charlotte? Mummy trod on her and hasn't said sorry!"

"Is Charlotte your secret friend?" smiled the ageing vicar.

"No I saw her today."

"And where was that?"

"Here... in this seat, silly!" cried Caroline, pointing directly at me.

"Mummy and I cannot see you friend. Why don't you tell me what she is wearing?"

I held my breath as the little girl looked me up and down briefly before turning back to the Vicar.

"Charlotte's got a long black dress on and it goes to her feet... she's got a black thing tied around her neck, it looks like a curtain!"

"Really? How interesting. Tell me Caroline, what colour is Charlotte's hair?"

"Er... brown!"

"And what does her hair look like?"

"It is very shiny and it goes down the middle."

"Well little girl, you are very observant! Perhaps you might ask Charlotte to go home with you for dinner?"

"Will you?" Caroline smiled at me, her eyes lighting up.

"No, little one, my meal is already awaiting me at my own home."

This message was duly related to the bespectacled old parson.

"Where does your friend live?" he asked, stooping over me to speak to the little girl.

"Tell him the Parsonage," I said cheekily, "My name is Charlotte Brontë!"

There was a complete uproar the moment Caroline carried out my order, and the reverend gentleman went quite pale! I decided to excuse myself for decency's sake but further commotion ensued when Caroline shouted that I had passed right through the church door without opening it!

"It's the ghost of the little lady!" one parishioner called out. Indeed, I had outstayed my welcome and escaped into the cemetery to watch folk spill out, looking wild.

I had been the cause of great consternation in church but as I watched the parishioners spilling from the building in a great panic, I felt light-hearted and a sense of mischief welled over me; for once, I did not care what I had done. For far too long I had been running and hiding from everyone. Now it did not matter – my secret was out – and folk were eager to get a glimpse of me. If I had suffered any embarrassment in the past I would not show it now, I felt quite proud of myself for being the centre of entertainment. Unfortunately, the means by which I had previously been made whole had now seemingly deserted me. It is typical of life that one strives to do good and be recognised, yet when death claims them they are denied this office. I was indeed more fortunate than most, to be able to come back to life periodically and enjoy all the attention. Now though, at the very pinnacle of being a famous and a much sought-after individual, Martha Clayton was denying me my moment of glory. However, better things were just on the horizon.

Within hours of my 'sighting' by the little girl in the church, both the newspapers and Mike had got wind of the story. He came to Haworth on a desperate mission to find me again. He was not on duty that weekend and the first I became aware of his presence was when I was looking in a shop window close to 'The Fleece' public house, lower down on Main Street. I caught his reflection in the glass as he walked by. I spun around and cried out his name but of course he could not hear me in my present form. I was devastated as I rushed after him and linked my arm through his. He was dressed casually in a pullover, shirt and jeans, his lovely bronze arms displayed from rolled up sleeves. (He later admitted that he had taken leave to lie down beneath a strange device known as a 'sun bed'. No wonder he was so tanned!)

Mike resolutely walked through the crowds with his firm jaw set solid and tenacity in his eyes, he seemed very intent on his mission. It was while I was studying him thus that I realised he was without facial hair. His 'Constantin' beard had gone! Oh – what sacrilege! – he had become a different man to the one I knew and loved. I was quite taken aback for a few moments but nevertheless he was still Mike, despite what he had done!

As we neared the top of Main Street, Mike withdrew a shiny little square object from his trouser pocket and proceeded to talk into it. I was quite intrigued by this action, having very little experience concerning the use of what you in this world refer to as mobile phones! I distinctly heard the voice of a female emanating from this box of tricks and Mike promising to be somewhere within a few moments. Crazily I was still holding on to his arm as we ascended the passageway by the church. In a few moments more we were inside St Michael's and walking up the aisle towards a group of people sat in quiet contemplation near the front of the steps by the eagle lectern. To my amazement I saw the face of little Caroline staring up at us as we approached, her mother and Joanna with her! Before I had time to think, Caroline jumped to her feet and excitedly pointed me out to the others!

"What?" cried Mike, turning to face me as I withdrew my arm from his, "Where is she?"

"Right next to you!" shouted Caroline, running up to me and patting my long dress. "You are very cold!" she exclaimed. I was truly shocked that, like in the last instance we met, Caroline's hands did not pass through me like one would normally expect – she found substance, but I know not how!

"Are you certain?" Mike cried out, trying to feel where I was.

"Yes, Charlotte is standing with her hands touching her mouth... she looks a bit scared of you!"

"Does she indeed? Charlotte? We know you are there, can you materialise?"

"Of course I cannot, you stupid fellow!" I mouthed, I felt quite annoyed to see Joanna sat there in this obviously arranged meeting with him. But who was the woman and child in relation to them?

"It's no use, Mike," called Joanna rising to her feet, "We will have to use Caroline as a mediator."

"How the hell can she see her when we can't?"

"I don't have an answer to that one, Mike. Maybe some of my gift has rubbed off on Caroline."

"Could be I suppose, what with you being her Aunt!" Mike grinned.

"Her Aunt?" I gasped. So now I understood; it would seem that Joanna had arranged this special meeting to consider the implications of my actions in the church. Obviously Mike had got into contact with Joanna when the story broke, but he must have been as shocked as I was when he learnt that Caroline and her mother were related to Joanna through her elder sister Rachel. To me this was doubly fascinating – if not a little frightening – knowing Caroline had the gift to see the unseen, far ahead of her Aunt Joanna! However, Mike was still not completely convinced Caroline could really see me, so he put forward a very personal question!

"Ask Charlotte if she remembers going into that old barn with me?"

Upon my soul, what a thing to ask an innocent five year old child! I looked down at Caroline and begged her to inform Mike that he ought to think first before opening his mouth on such a delicate subject! This was duly passed on, but in her own way.

"Charlotte says you shouldn't talk about naughty things in front of me!"

"Really? Ask her what she means exactly?"

Caroline turned back to me, her little cherub face all agog and her eyes wide with expectation.

"Please inform Mike that we are fortunate that the farmer did not catch us rolling in the hay!"

"Charlotte said a man nearly caught you playing in the straw with her. What were you playing? Can we play now?"

"Never you mind, young lady!" Mike laughed but I could see he was deeply shocked, knowing now that I really were present in their midst. Joanna let forth a giggle and cupped a hand over her mouth. Caroline's mother looked quite disgusted.

"I reckon we ought to step outside and continue this conversation in more quiet surroundings?" suggested Mike.

"Agreed," Joanna nodded, looking around at the other visitors to the church.

Once outside we all trooped towards the little iron turnstile that marked the beginning of the paths leading towards the moors. As we passed the grave of Martha Clayton I stopped and communicated, through little Caroline, my wish to see the old woman silenced forever.

"It has already been done Charlotte," smiled Joanna.

"Before Marie left for home she carried out a service over the grave; Martha Clayton no longer has any power over you."

"Upon my soul!" I cried out, "No wonder I have not been able to appear to her or Mike. Does this mean I am now doomed to walk forever unseen?"

"Yes, Charlotte, I'm afraid it does," nodded Joanna when Caroline eagerly passed my words on.

"It's for the best, love," agreed Mike, finding Joanna's hand and clasping it firmly.

In that moment, Reader, my heart broke. I knew that I had lost my young gentleman forever. The hurt was overwhelming but I knew that I had to face the truth, and I wished them both well in their lives together.

I had been the means of bringing two young people together and sealing their future happiness. As a woman though, I could not but feel pain knowing that the man I loved had taken his feelings away from me to bring joy into the life of another female. When Joanna asked me if I still wanted to continue the walk, I declined. I sadly informed the little group that my mission on earth had now been completed and I was of no further use to them.

"Goodbye then Charlotte," said Joanna, trying to feel my presence when guided by Caroline.

Mike put his arm on her shoulder, smiled briefly in my direction, then turned to go. The others followed as tears welled up in my eyes and I held them under observation until they were out of sight. Finally, I looked down at the grave of my tormentor.

"Sleep on, Martha Clayton, you were sadly mistaken if you thought Good would never triumph over Evil... I am yet free to go where I please and be happy; you will remain a prisoner of your evil master forever. May the Lord take mercy upon your wretched soul!"

The End